Road Trip

(*Fashion and Fiends*, book four)

by Angel Ackerman

Road Trip
Copyright 2024 by Angel R. Ackerman
Print 978-1-957863-24-5
Ebook 978-1-957863-25-2

Angel R. Ackerman
angel@parisianphoenix.com

Published by Parisian Phoenix Publishing, Easton, Pennsylvania USA

Author Photo: Joan Zachary, joanzachary.com
Cover photo: JLGutierrez/istockphoto.com

C O N N E C T with the publisher:
 ParisianPhoenix
 ParisBirdBooks
 parisianphoenix

C O N N E C T with the author:
 bit.ly/3s6R8Ln
 AngelAckerman
 angelackerman
 creatively angel

NOVELS BY ANGEL ACKERMAN

The Fashion and Fiends series
Manipulations
Courting Apparitions
Road Trip
Absolution, anticipated 2025
Finding Hooyo, anticipated 2025

Other stories about Jules:
Not the Quiet French Kid

NON-FICTION EDITED AS ANGEL R. ACKERMAN

Not an Able-Bodied White Man with Money:
Expressions of Alternative Perspectives Influenced
by Experiences in Lehigh Valley, Pennsylvania

EROTICA EDITED AS ANGEL ACKERMAN

Juicy Bits. Erotic Stories of BDSM, Kink and Fetish (with Ralph Greco Jr.)

DEDICATION:

To Eva

Still in the midst of her own coming of age story

March 2003

CHAPTER ONE

Water dripped from the air conditioner onto the carpet. The ceiling fan rattled as it spun. The room hadn't cooled, but at least the moisture in the air no longer choked him. Jules peeled off the army-issue, sandy-colored t-shirt, kicked away the unfamiliar ranger boots, discarded the socks, and shimmied out of the leopard print fatigue pants—not even sure what had happened to the boxers.

He headed straight for the bathroom, only a step from the hotel room door. Jules met his reflection in the mirror: sunburned, exhausted, black hair tinted "blond" from the dust of his travels. He pulled the hair tie from his ratty ponytail, unleashing dry and sandy waves to his shoulders. He ran his hand across his stubbled jaw line.

How the Hell did all of this happen? Merely days ago, he was helping his wealthy employer, Basilie Saint-Ebène d'Amille, and her family settle into their Parisian apartment with their infant. Two months ago, they had been in the United States with hopes of cocktail parties and a newborn child to puncture the depression of Basilie's husband, flighty fashion magnate Étienne d'Amille. Three months ago, Jules was wearing chef whites in the kitchen of an up-and-coming Parisian restaurant, where Étienne loved the langoustines.

He started the shower in this ramshackle hotel. He dreamed of hot water, but in downtown Djibouti there were no hot water heaters. With the sun always shining, 90 percent humidity, and an average temperature of 32 degrees Celsius, heating water for a shower meant wasting energy in a developing nation. The shampoo on the edge of the sink featured black tint, which he might be able to use with his natural hair color, and the soap... well, one didn't get luxuries in this hotel despite its status as one of the nicer places in the neighborhood.

Jules stepped under the shower, merely a fixture extending from the wall with no enclosure and a flimsy shower curtain pretending to create a barrier. Small white tiles covered the whole room except for the ceiling. The room temperate water pelted him, sprinkling beyond the minimal border, and headed toward the drain in the middle of the bathroom floor.

Before this, he had traveled to a few places in France, Germany and the United States, primarily places where his extended family lived or where his culinary school internships and later career had sent him. This was Africa, hardcore Africa.

He arrived here via a hole in the sky. He chuckled. Not exactly. But that's certainly how it felt and how it looked.

One minute he had just arrived home in the Paris apartment he hadn't seen in a few months, about to kick off his shoes. The next minute, a gleaming sliver of light appeared in his living area and a petite Asian woman stepped from it. Before he could finish a sigh of dread/ emotional fatigue, she bowed to him and uttered the phrase he really did not want to hear.

"We have to go," Jaing said. "I am sorry, but Kait needs you."

In addition to his plebeian life as an executive chef, he had what one might consider an unpaid side gig. As if being a 26-year-old chef working eighty hours a week didn't offer enough challenges, he had inherited a supernatural calling— he served as "protector" for the "guardian" of "water power," an orange-haired Irish preteen roughly 1.5 meters tall and 400-years-old. He received this unique position six years ago when apparently his predecessor had died. He still didn't understand it all. He approached it as the metaphysical equivalent of punching a time clock and going home.

Jaing, the sinewy warrior who served as the fire guardian, grabbed his arm. The portal reappeared and she leapt into it, dragging him to an unknown destination with no more preparation or direction other than that meek apology.

So now, his "job" as protector had provided him with a free, bonus vacation to Djibouti. But he didn't have a passport to get home.

As he worked the strange shampoo into his hair, it didn't lather. It had a texture more like lard. When he couldn't rinse it out, he ran the small bar of soap across his head. The water and soap ran across the fresh scratches on his back. He closed his eyes as his body fought an erection. The recent unexpected proximity and availability of someone who trusted him and desired him had led to a spontaneous tryst, totally out-of-character for him. He trembled, absorbing the sensation as he didn't know if he wanted to cum or cry— life had gotten that weird.

He leaned against the wall, the water still caressing his back. The vaguely cool texture of the tile sunk into his forehead but did nothing to quiet the passion building as he replayed the memories from a few hours earlier.

After what had happened when his fiancée left him—part of the upheaval in his life six years ago—he had sworn off sex, and now he had reneged on his promise to himself. The combination of nurturing persona, alluring body, and feisty spirit made it impossible to resist her. They fucked violently like animals in the rear bed of an army supply truck. Even now, in the relatively inhospitable conditions of the Horn of Africa, the vibrations of her touch lingering on his skin, her smell stuck in his nose and the unforgettable power of an orgasm while securely nestled in a welcoming woman... the replay from the depth of his mind made him ready to do it again, but there would be no again.

The plumbing squealed. The water stopped. Jules opened his eyes and peered to the shower head. He adjusted the taps. Nothing.

"Let me guess," he grumbled. "The hotel has run out of water."

Each building in Djibouti had a tank and got water delivered. When it was gone, it was gone until the next delivery. Jules trotted to his bed, wet feet across thin carpet already soggy from the humidity. He retrieved a 16.9-ounce bottle of water from the nightstand. He had to fight a handful of tiny, scurrying cockroaches for it. Of course, he could have purchased the one-liter bottle yesterday, but he didn't. He bought the small one. He brought what remaining water he had to the bathroom and used it to wash off the soap, praying to whatever creative forces running the show that they would allow him to finish bathing.

Hopefully, tomorrow DHL would deliver his passport and he could leave this shit hole. His boss— well his traditional boss and his supernatural boss, so his bosses—had disappeared. He knew he had to find them, but he also sensed they were no longer here. He had lost their scent after Ghoubbet.

That's when his boss's sister-in-law (the traditional boss, not the minuscule Irish one; the sister-in-law who worked for the French Army Health Service—Principal Doctor Jacqueline Saint-Ebène) found him dehydrated, naked, and sunburnt amidst the rocky countryside near an abandoned nomad village where she and her unit were building a combat support hospital as a training exercise.

Somehow, they started touching each other, and one thing led to another.

He wrapped a towel around his waist, not that he was very wet, and started toward the hard twin bed.

Jacqueline Saint-Ebène scared him, and not because she was ten years older than him and a combat surgeon.

Lying on the bed, towel still around his waist, he tried to think of anything that might ease his discomfort below the waist. Her scent, and not just her body odor, but her female reproductive smell, covered him. It laid on his skin like the salt of the ocean after a good surf.

Cacophonous banging assailed him from his hotel room door.

Jules' body jerked. His current arousal had allowed someone to sneak up on him. That normally didn't happen. He shook off the surprise and inhaled. Even without the dramatic, overzealous knocking he recognized the scent of Didier Robineau, Étienne's second-in-command and best friend.

"Jules!" Didier said, in a constrained voice that so clearly indicated that he resisted screaming. "Jules! Are you in there?"

Jules sat up and peeled himself off the bed. He went to grab his pants. Then, he realized he had left them outside. Outside the town.

"Just a sec," he muttered.

The dirty fatigues laid on the bathroom floor, now wet from the shower drainage.

"Hey, Didier," he called through the door. "Can you find me some clothes?"

"Now, Jules? Now?"

"I have a towel, Didier, and a borrowed Army uniform that's dripping wet."

"Well, that sounds like a story," Didier muttered as he departed.

Didier's footsteps headed toward the hotel's central stairwell. Jules sighed. He should have also asked for a toothbrush. While he waited, he braided his hair. Thought it better for long-term upkeep versus his usual ponytail. Didier returned relatively quickly, Jules wondered if he went to the European business casual-style clothing store next to the hotel.

Jules opened the door before Didier had a chance to knock. Didier handed him a dark purple square of fabric.

"It's a futa," Didier said. "Between the heat and how tall you are, I found it the safest option without you present."

Jules opened it. The futa resembled a woman's wrap-around skirt.

"It's a skirt," he said.

"Less restrictive than pants, too," Didier said.

"How thoughtful," Jules said dryly.

He wrapped the fabric around his waist and dropped his towel.

"I confirmed that Étienne and Kait were at Ghoubbet," Jules said.

"I know," Didier said, "Étienne came back with Kait this morning."

"Oh that's a relief," Jules said.

"Not really," Didier replied. "Apparently, he got attacked by the monster who lives in Ghoubbet. So I made him go to the hospital. To find Jacqueline."

"Jacqueline's not at Bouffard..." Jules said on auto-pilot. He repeated the sentence Didier had said silently to himself. "Wait. What monster?"

"From the descriptions I heard, it sounded like the Loch Ness monster or a dinosaur, but I never saw it."

"Seriously?" Jules said with his full Generation X incredulous tone.

"You know the translation of Ghoubbet means 'Devil's Goblet,'" Didier reported.

"I did not know," he said.

Jules tried to picture a dinosaur hiding in Ghoubbet. That lake really didn't seem deep enough to harbor such a creature. Jules shook his head. Only he would consider the logistics of a Ghoubbet monster versus the reality of it. Because he knew something supernatural could exist in the lake, and he knew, at this point, it could be anything.

"Is there room for a monster in the lake?" Jules asked.

Didier chuckled. Jules recoiled a bit, taken aback that Didier implied a certain idiocy to his Djibouti knowledge.

"It's not a lake," Didier corrected Jules. "It is a cove amidst the volcano that opens to the Gulf of Tadjourah."

"Ah, forgive my ignorance," Jules replied.

"And you know, Jacques Cousteau himself discovered the monster, when it stole a dead camel that they had submerged—"

"This is starting to sound like a script by Jean Cocteau," Jules interrupted. "So Étienne's at Bouffard, again?"

"No," Didier said.

"He's here in the hotel?"

"No," Didier said.

"Then where is he? Where's Kait?"

"They left Djibouti," Didier said. "Neferkaba warned us that the were-wolves are coming, and he got the idea that Africa wasn't the place for the epic showdown."

"The spirit guardian warned you... werewolves coming..." This latest development made it hard for Jules to think straight. "But... I'm already here. You don't think..."

Didier said nothing.

"We're going to need a better plan, or a plan, any plan," Jules finally said.

"Let me check my luggage and see if I have a t-shirt for you," Didier said. "Meet you in the lobby?"

Jules sighed. "Sure."

Clothes no longer seemed so vital. Didier left the room again.

Jules wanted to say, "Sure, Didier, I'll wander around half-naked in the hot, African sun while you treat me like a search-and-rescue dog."

But he didn't. He instead considered going to get his real clothes. When Didier insisted that Étienne and Kait had gone to Ghoubbet, he had taken a cab to the lake and then removed his clothes before transforming. At the time, he hadn't anticipated getting intercepted by the French Army. And he certainly didn't anticipate an afternoon tryst with a doctor. At a combat hospital.

Jules had earned his role as protector of the water guardian because his family carried a gene with latent wolf DNA merged with human. In Jules, the wolf gene had activated, making him a chimera and a werewolf.

A familiar, bright light filled the room. The light tightened into a slit, vivid and vibrant. Before he could fully think "oh no," two women fell from it.

The first woman was taller than average and thin, and muscular for a girl, with dark hair and dark eyes. She wore streamlined jeggings and a lightweight sweater in magenta with quarter-length sleeves that draped to the tops of her thighs. Her hair fell across her face in haphazard waves, but it couldn't disguise her identity. His sister. She obviously hadn't been expecting to travel as she didn't have shoes, only a black pair of ankle-height, crew socks.

"What the hell, Minette?" Jules exclaimed.

Beside her stood Jaing. Minette had recently been activated as the fire protector, just as he worked for Kait as the water protector. Minette folded at the waist and heaved onto the already soggy carpet. Jaing dotingly pulled Minette's hair from her face so she didn't puke on it. The guardians could travel via strange portals, but humans who accompanied them never fared well. He himself had learned to hold his breath and hope for the best.

"Jaing, Min, what's going on?"'

But he already knew. It's as Neferkaba told Didier. (Neferkaba was the Spirit Guardian, the overseer of the guardians who protected the four creative elements of magick.) So this is what she meant.

The werewolves had arrived, despite the fact that his sister shouldn't be a werewolf. Jules' father, the prestigious genetic researcher and medical doctor Dr. Benedict Zweigenbaum had insisted that the "lycanthropic seizure disorder" could not appear in females as it required a Y chromosome and certain levels of testosterone to trigger a full transformation. Therefore, females could only be carriers of this recessive condition. They hadn't revealed Min's secret yet.

Minette exhaled and wiped her mouth with the back of her hand. Jules passed her his towel. She grimaced. He passed her a bottle of water Didier had left behind. She gulped half of it. Color slowly returned to her face.

"I sure would like to know what's going on," she said. "I was working on the last paper that stood between me and spring break and all of a sudden Jaing was throwing me into that hole. Where are we?"

She tossed an engineering textbook on the floor. The picture on its cover showed fancy bridges over water.

"Djibouti," Jules answered.

He stared at the book.

"I repeat, where are we?" Her voice sounded shrill.

"Djibouti, former French colony. East Africa. Borders Somalia and Ethiopia. Don't you remember?" he asked.

"Remember? You expect me to remember French colonial history? We moved to the United States when I was still in elementary school. I barely speak French," she replied.

"The Spirit Guardian has asked us to find Kait and the Frenchman," Jaing said softly. "They are in danger. The world is in danger. I have brought your sister to help you. Neferkaba has asked the twin protectors to find the errant water guardian and the sire to the offspring."

Jules rolled those words across his mind.

"The twin protectors?" Minette said.

Errant water guardian was Kait, but what was Étienne's role as "sire to the offspring?" His infant son, Alèxandre?

"We're more than six years apart," Minette said. "Not even remotely twins."

Didier returned and walked into the room waving a white tee shirt. He froze when he saw that there were new people in the room. Jules grabbed the shirt, slipping his arms into it.

"Didier, I believe you've met my sister, Minette."

"I have," he said, pulling her into a casual set of bisous, one cheek and then the other. She had pimples and patches of healing acne on her jawline. "But I do not know—"

He moved toward Jaing, extending his arm for a handshake. Jaing drew her sword. Jules hadn't seen where she had a sword.

"I am Jaing, guardian of fire, sent by Neferkaba, the Spirit Guardian, to assign the twin protectors to their duty of appeasing the stray water guardian before the carrier bears the offspring."

"Whoa," Didier said, withdrawing the hand he had offered. "I'm Didier Robineau. I came to Djibouti hoping to find answers about why I'm quasi-psychic after an accident here twenty-five years ago."

"The twin protectors have a job to do, seeking the sire and the errant guardian," Jaing repeated.

"She means Étienne and Kait," Jules explained. "I'm guessing my sister and I are the werewolves in question. But, Didier, didn't you say that Étienne had left the country?"

Didier stood in the middle of the room, eyebrows twisting as his eyes moved from Jules to Minette.

"Sibling werewolves?" he said.

"Didier, where did Étienne go?" Jules asked.

"France," Didier answered.

"Jaing, can you transport us to Paris?" Jules asked, dreading a trip through the portal.

"Hard no," Minette said. "I'm not getting in one of those swirly light holes again."

"I cannot take the unblessed one," Jaing replied.

"Unblessed?" Jules repeated.

"Nothing about this feels like a blessing," Minette said.

The sword danced above Jaing's head. She sheathed it as a white zipper of light appeared.

"I'll stay here," Didier said. "Don't they always leave someone behind in case the person in question comes back?"

Jules reached for Jaing's hand. Jaing wrapped her fingers around Minette's wrist and the world went white with heat and swirling energy. Jules missed his life as a chef.

CHAPTER TWO

Minette closed the door of the water closet in his small Paris apartment. Jules stood frozen in the living room as Jaing disappeared. Did Minette realize that he could hear her soft whimpers? He didn't know if it were better to give her space or try and comfort her. After all, she wasn't six anymore. And she might need a minute to comprehend everything. She might need a year or two. He might need a year or two.

Jules closed his eyes and absorbed the familiar smells: the dusty plaster walls, a lingering far scent of alcohol and urine— not from him, or Min, or even his toilet, but from the street, several stories below them. He slowly moved into his bedroom. As he did, the weight of fatigue crashed into him.

His father had always said that only biological males could transform into wolves— that girls couldn't become actual werewolves. Never in his research nor his medical practice had Dr. Zweigenbaum found a female werewolf.

And then Jules' sister turns up a month ago, insisting she could change into a wolf. And she didn't know what to do. As if Jules had an answer. Or a training manual for newly-minted werewolves. At the time, Jules was dealing with a supernatural psychopath. In his role as protector of water magick, he had to leave his grueling chef job here in Paris to serve as private chef for flaky fashion designer, Étienne d'Amille. But then Minette showed him the tattoo that had appeared on her shoulder, the gold-flecked flame, and he knew she had bigger problems. The tattoo matched his silver-lined water droplet. How could she be a werewolf, and with only a handful of elemental guardians, how could a sister and brother both end up called to protect them?

Present-day Jules grabbed clean underwear, a t-shirt and sweats (in homage to Minette's arrival, he opted for his Lafayette College sweats; that's where she studied engineering) from his bureau and changed. He stretched across the bed.

Minette sobbed now. He heard it so clearly. But then he also heard her gurgling his Listerine. Minette wandered out of the bathroom. She found him as she surveyed his bedroom. He didn't have much: a bureau, a double bed, some curtains hiding the Parisian landscape, and a coat tree which contained some white chef jackets.

"So this is France," she stated in English.

"Yeah," he answered in French.

"I thought I saw C and F on the sink," she replied, also in French. "In Paris?"

"Yes," he said.

"I've never been to Paris," she said.

He moved his arm, propping himself up. They were all born in France.

"Really?"

She nodded. "Biarritz, of course, to see family, but never Paris."

"I will show you around," he said.

"What do we do now?" she asked.

Minette swept her hand along the top of his bureau. She lifted a photo of them: Jules, Minette and their older brother, Benji. Benji had escaped this nonsense. Benji had attempted a career as a professional surfer and then procured a position as a bartender in a shady fish-and-chips place on the boardwalk.

"We sleep," Jules replied.

He pointed to the top drawer of his bureau.

"Grab something comfortable and come to bed. If Étienne and Kait are on a plane, we can catch up with them in the morning. It's an eight-hour flight. I haven't slept in days."

She obeyed, retrieving another t-shirt and pair of sweatpants. He had a lot of sweats. He blamed it on his American side. She did not pick Lafayette gear. She decided on a green t-shirt and generic gray pants instead.

"Where am I going to sleep?" she asked, holding the clothes to her chest.

"Right here," he answered.

"I'm not sleeping in your bed, Jules," she said.

"You're my sister. We're both nearly two meters tall. You can't sleep on the couch. Besides, I only have a loveseat."

Minette scowled.

"Sleep wherever you prefer," he said.

She returned to the bathroom. She quickly changed and walked back to her brother's bedroom.

"Are you scared?" she asked in a voice he hadn't heard since she was a little girl.

"Of you? Sleeping in my bed?"

She rolled her eyes as sat beside him.

"Annoyed, maybe, but not afraid," he told her.

"I don't understand any of this," she said.

"Honestly," he responded, "neither do I. I've merely accepted it."

He took her hand in his.

"It's okay, Min," he said softly. "We're in this together. Now please, go the fuck to sleep."

She turned down the covers and slipped into bed. He was still on top of the blankets.

"Min, I know you're not really into this," Jules said. "But if we have to do this, then I'm really glad I can spend time with you…"

God, did this all sound lame. He suppressed the urge to sigh.

"…And maybe, together, we can master this werewolf thing."

The energy in the room suddenly grew heavier. The silence seemed infinite. Then, she started to speak, but the words at first sounded like strangled chirps.

"I haven't told Dad."

"Still?" he blurted.

"Still," she admitted. "You know Dad. He'll ask me to do all sorts of medical tests and put me on drugs. And I still remember how he treated you when you changed… you became a project. And he feared you. He's my daddy. I don't want him to be afraid of me."

Suddenly, she started sobbing into the pillow. Jules sighed.

"Min," he said. "You're 'daddy's little girl.' You will always be the favorite."

They were both too tired to talk anymore. Jules never even made it under the blankets. Sleep consumed him with otherworldly depth, and he didn't have the energy to dream.

As the sun gently slid its glow into the narrow break in the curtain, Minette slept peacefully, her body curled ever-so-slightly into a hint of the fetal position. Jules extracted himself from the bedroom with instinctual precision, not making an unnecessary movement or sound, as he meandered to the bathroom and then the kitchen. He filled the kettle with fresh water. Assessing recent events and his guest, he opted for a rich, strong coffee from his press.

He should check on Madame Basilie d'Amille. Regardless of her opinion about his role in Étienne's behavior, she probably needed breakfast, moral support, and should get and/or have an update. Worst case scenario, she would throw him out.

Grinding the beans released their aroma. He transferred the coffee into the bottom of the carafe and filled it with hot water. He glanced at the clock, setting a mental timer. While the coffee brewed, he gathered mugs and for his sister, sugar. He calculated the age of the milk still in his fridge, and deeming it good enough for now, he warmed some on the stove. He also frothed it, because why not?

He brought both finished coffees into the bedroom.

"Min?" he greeted her.

If she hadn't heard him in the kitchen, she had to have heard the coffee grinder. She bolted up.

"Good morning," he handed her the coffee.

She pulled it close and sipped it.

"How do you know how I like my coffee?" she asked.

"You're a college student," he said.

They drank coffee silently.

"I think I will go see Madame. She might know where Étienne is."

"Has she forgiven you?"

Jules just stood there. He didn't know what to say. Had Madame recovered from other recent events? Jules had witnessed Étienne's unfortunate, sexual encounter with Kait, though Jules did not anticipate that Kait would seduce Étienne. He supposed it made sense. This whole recent mess started because a ghost had moved into Étienne's body. The ghost of Adelaide Pitney, a whiny supermodel who for some reason served as Étienne's muse, used Étienne as a secret hiding spot and Kait thought sex would draw her out. The physics seemed reasonable. But Madame found out and blamed Jules.

At least, that's how it looked.

"I take that as a no," Minette finally said. "Do you want me to come?"

"Why?" Jules asked.

Minette shrugged without lowering the mug from her lips.

"I'm not sure," she said. "But sometimes having another woman around helps."

"You're not wrong," Jules said.

CHAPTER THREE

J ules balanced the sacks of groceries as he shoved his hand into his pocket for his key ring. One of them opened this door. He debated whether or not it would be appropriate to use his key— because Madame did not exactly terminate him, but she did command him to "get out" the last time he saw her. While he lingered, Minette leaned forward and pressed the doorbell.

Jules and his employer had not clarified the situation before his impromptu departure for Djibouti. Minette rang the doorbell a second time. When Jules had texted Madame earlier, Basilie had asked him to bring food as her grandmother-in-law planned to make *pil-pil*.

"Paris is fancy," Minette said randomly, "but surprisingly stinky and dirty."

Jules chuckled. "It is."

He didn't know if Minette had intended to break the tension. He had suspected she did. Jules heard stocking-feet footfalls beyond the door, and he knew Minette could hear them, too. He wondered if Minette had started to notice the phantom smells on people, for example the delicate traces of soap or the activation of an antiperspirant. Because even now, Jules could smell Madame's toiletries and breast milk. He could often smell people coming before he heard them. The door opened.

Madame Basilie Saint-Ébène d'Amille stood before them, hair in a bun with tendrils flailing, face stoic with tight lips and tired eyes. She held the baby— Jules did the math in his head, Alèx was a little more than four weeks old now— in her arm to the right side. The infant cooed drowsily.

"Madame," Jules said.

"Madame," Minette also said.

"Jules, Minette," Basilie replied.

She swept her arm across the threshold as an invitation. They proceeded into the apartment.

"You have a key," Basilie said.

"It seemed rude," Jules responded. "I'm not even sure if I have a job."

"Valid point," Basilie said.

He lifted the bag of groceries.

"Can we talk in the kitchen? I'll make breakfast," Jules said.

Basilie nodded. Jules led the way.

"And what do you have against *pil-pil?*" he asked. "Done well... Better than a scampi. The *guindilla* in tandem with the garlic... Does Étienne's grandmother use traditional clay cookware?"

"You're into Basque cuisine?" Basilie responded.

"I lived in Biarritz until I was fourteen," Jules said. "So my culinary influences are French, American, Basque and Spanish. There's a bean dish with the *guindilla*..."

They had reached the kitchen.

"Oh, I hate that!" Basilie exclaimed. "I know the one. She makes it with cabbage."

Jules smiled. "That's it."

"*Alubias,*" Minette replied.

Jules glanced to Minette, hoping she would give him some sort of signal if he were babbling. She seemed indifferent, or perhaps mesmerized by the European lines of the Place des Vosges apartment. Jules arranged a bottle of milk, a carton of eggs, butter, honey, some strawberries, something wrapped in butcher paper and a package of American-style sandwich bread on the counter.

"Your speech is greatly improved," Jules said.

Basilie had had a stroke earlier this year, thanks to a rather dramatic, supernatural lover Adelaide had taken. Long story, and if Jules survived all of this, he might write a book about it.

Jules pulled spice bottles out of the grocery bag, nutmeg and cinnamon.

"I talk to myself often," Basilie replied.

That ruptured Jules' daydream of sitting at a typewriter, which was probably good because he couldn't even decide what language to use— his native French or English?

Minette stood to the side, studying the details of the kitchen and inching toward the next room.

"There's a sauce... normally used for rabbit," Jules said, a light and whimsical air in his voice. "It's a blend of *mole* and *crème fraiche*. It uses *guindilla* and chocolate. Have you had it?"

He really should stop talking about regional French cuisine.

"I don't think I have," Basilie said.

"Ask Grandmother. I bet she can make it," Jules said. "I have a recipe for it, but it wouldn't be the same."

"What are you making?" Basilie asked.

The next bottle in Jules' line-up contained strawberry jam.

"Something different," he answered.

Simplicity, sweetness, the exotic use of American recipes in a French kitchen. Jules reached into Basilie's cupboard, grabbing the familiar cast iron skillet and placing it on the stove. He gathered a mixing bowl, a whisk, a small knife and a smaller bowl. He sliced a hearty amount of butter into the skillet, setting the flame low. He poured milk into the larger bowl. He rolled an egg into his right hand, cracked it on the counter, and separated the shell with his fingers. He did this with several more eggs. Once he plopped them into the larger bowl, he whisked them into the milk. The skillet sizzled.

"Did you see Étienne?" he asked her.

Jules grabbed the package of meat. He took it to the stove. He unwrapped some sausage links and dropped them into the hot skillet.

"Yes, briefly. Last night," Basilie said.

That soon? Jules thought about the math. They must have made good time in the air. "Was Kait with him?"

"No," Basilie said.

Jules sprinkled cinnamon, nutmeg and a dash of vanilla bean into his egg mix.

"They had to have left Djibouti together," Jules said.

"He came alone," Basilie said, "and he did not stay. He went to Chicago, chasing Adelaide again. I asked him not to—"

"Chicago?" Jules interrupted.

Jules wondered if Kait would further desecrate Adelaide's grave. He had a slice of American bread in each hand.

"So it was them," Jules said to Minette.

He dipped the bread into the milk.

"Now I am really confused," Basilie said. "What are you making? Because wet bread does not seem an appropriate breakfast, nor does it look appealing."

Jules added the soggy bread to the skillet beside the sausages.

"Seriously?" Jules said. "The end of that got jumbled, but your confusion is noted. It's French toast. A classic. You didn't figure that out?"

"I don't cook. Ever. And while I am French, I certainly would have no idea how to make this 'French toast' which looks suspiciously American."

"I am true to my roots," Jules said in a stage-whisper.

Minette slid to his side and sliced strawberries.

"Thanks, Min," Jules said. "Something happened in Chicago. The magick was unbelievably strong. Water magick, mixed with fire. Neferkaba said she'd deal with it. The fire guardian volunteered to go, but Neferkaba said no."

"If Jaing would have gone," Minette said, "we would have gone, too."

"Wait," Basilie said. "Your sister? How is she—"

Jules inhaled.

"Involved?" Jules finished. "Don't tell my dad."

Just how much should Basilie know?

"She got the werewolf gene," Jules said. "And she can change. Which girls aren't supposed to be able to do. Werewolves help the guardians. Sometimes protectors. Sometimes enforcers. Minette was called to assist Jaing, as I was assigned to Kait."

"You work for Kait? While you've been..." the words switched to a language Jules didn't understand. It sounded angry. It sounded German.

"Ma'am," Minette interrupted. "You've changed languages."

Jules arranged two slices of French toast on his wooden turner, sliding them onto the plate beside three sausage links.

"I've been paying you, rather well, and you've been working for her."

The tone in Basilie's voice had sharpened, and she struggled not to jostle the baby.

"Not working in the modern capitalist society way," he said. "More against-my-will, supernatural calling. Think *Buffy The Vampire Slayer.*"

She stared blanking at him, but at least Minette nodded thoughtfully. Jules should have known Madame would not know Buffy. He adorned the bread with sliced strawberries, drizzled honey on the French toast, scooped a dollop of jam into the center and circled that with more sliced strawberries. He presented Basilie with the artfully-plated breakfast and then handed her a fork. He continued cooking the next set.

"What is happening now?" Basilie asked.

With the baby on her hip as she leaned over the central island, she scooped the first taste of French toast into her mouth. She moaned softly. Jules smirked from behind his skillet. He still had the touch.

"Neferkaba is dead," Minette said.

Leave it to Minette to keep the conversation on the business at hand. Sometimes, Jules wanted to enjoy a meal in peace.

"Isn't that the god that blinded Étienne?" Basilie asked.

"You heard about that?" Jules replied. "Yes. She was the leader. Her job is to keep the creative powers of the universe in check."

He didn't know how to explain it. He didn't even understand it.

"Creative powers?" Basilie repeated. "Is she God? Allah God or Father Son and Holy Spirit God? Jehovah?"

With her fancy acacia turner gently swaying in his hand, he shrugged. He didn't understand any of it, not really.

"I don't know," Jules said. "I don't think so."

He flipped the French toast he had in the pan for his sister.

"But she died?" Basilie asked.

Well, Jules thought with a slight exhale, how best to explain it... He gazed into the depths of the flame beneath the cast iron.

"She shares a connection with the others, and they say she's gone."

"So who's in charge now?" Basilie asked.

Good question. Jules shrugged, his attention still on the stove.

"No one," he said.

"And whatever happened... happened in Chicago..." Basilie said.

Her stroke accent intensified as the emotion rolled over her face, a sadness sunk her cheeks and snuffed the light from her eyes. The baby gurgled.

"I wish I could say I didn't believe Étienne was involved," Jules said.

Jules passed his sister a plate and started a third batch. Basilie stood. She set her plate on the counter beside the sink. She leaned against the counter, facing both of them, not far from Jules, and slipped her now free hand under her shirt. Next, she rolled Alèxandre under the fabric and the baby suckled as Basilie held him against her belly.

"What next?" Basilie asked. "If you have this job, working for them, why did you become a chef?"

Jules pivoted. As if he had a choice. He had the final plate of French toast in his grasp. He clicked off the burner.

"I don't understand this any more than you do," he said. He stared at the pan with downcast eyes. "I hate it."

"What if you refuse?"

Jules shrugged. "I may not have to. My obligation ends with Kait. If she... no longer... I'm free. I think."

He set his plate on the island.

"Jules, did you really try to stop them?" Basilie asked.

What was she asking? Stop who? Then, it hit him.

"Kait and Étienne?"

Basilie did not meet his eyes— she fumbled under her shirt, placing the baby into a better position. Basilie seemed to contort herself uncomfortably, but as the hired help, he didn't know how best to help. Minette, meanwhile, used the last of her bread to sop up the juices on her plate.

"Yes," Basilie confirmed.

Did she understand there were mystical forces at work? Because she kept asking for details he didn't know. But he knew what Kait had told him.

"Yes. If I'd have left her finish, this mess would have never happened. You wouldn't have had a stroke. Étienne wouldn't have dug up Addy's corpse or run off to Djibouti... We need to find them."

Basilie moved into the dining room. She peered over her shoulder and motioned for Jules to follow. He did, as did Minette. Basilie led them to her computer. She powered the machine.

"Shouldn't be a problem," Basilie replied. "Étienne is bad at being sneaky. I'll check the charge card accounts. He had to pay for something by now."

In what seemed like seconds, she had pointed out several transactions that proved Étienne had indeed gone to Chicago.

"If you could track him this easily, why didn't you?" Jules asked.

"It's been eight hours," Basilie said, in English this time. "I was unaware he was missing."

Basilie read the statement to them. The most recent charge to Étienne's corporate card indicated an AirFrance purchase. The price tag suggested several first class tickets on a transcontinental flight, Basilie noted. Next, she found several thousand dollars in charges at Marshall Fields and a hold from The Peninsula Hotel.

"Viola," Basilie said.

"I'll bring him home," Jules said.

Basilie's phone buzzed within her pocket. She handed the printed out, credit card statement to Jules. He accepted the paper. She retrieved her phone and read an incoming text message. She pecked a few words to respond, leaving the Blackberry on the table. Amidst it all, the baby kept nursing.

"Do you think I could have another helping?" Basilie asked.

"Sure," Jules said. He turned to Minette. "And you?"

"Heck yeah," Minette said.

At least for a few more hours, he could relax and focus on being a chef.

CHAPTER FOUR

Chicago. That seemed to be the answer. The logical place to go.

Back in his apartment, Jules organized the few groceries he purchased for himself as Minette showered. The groceries seemed completely superfluous now if he needed to return to the United States. How on Earth would they get to Chicago? Didier had just received Jules' passport in Djibouti and now had to return it to Paris. It should arrive at the Chez d'Amille offices tomorrow. But Minette... Her passport might be in her college dorm or it might be at home. Would he have to call Mom and Dad?

The shower had stopped— honestly despite the puzzling and nonsensical situation, suddenly bathing with real hot water and familiar soap sounded like exactly what he needed. Minette emerged from the bathroom, her hair wet, her face refreshed and wearing another of Jules' t-shirts with a pair of dark jeans they had purchased on the walk home from Madame's apartment.

"You okay?" Jules asked as he left the kitchen, and joined her in the tiny living room. Nothing really separated the two rooms, except for an awkward nub of counter that extended briefly toward the love seat.

"Yeah," she said.

She lowered herself to the couch with an exaggerated slowness as if she had aged forty years in the last day.

"Maybe," she said, changing her answer. "Is it just me, or could it be that Dad has no clue what this werewolf stuff is all about?"

Jules chuckled. "Dad's a doctor. To him, it's a chromosomal abnormality. If we told him that people could use magick and that there were special people to protect it and that we protected them... Well, he'd never believe us."

"Are there only four werewolves in the world?" Minette asked.

"I don't know," Jules said. "I think there are more of us, but not all of us do the same thing."

"Like there are werewolf jobs? A werewolf aptitude test?"

He chuckled.

"Maybe. I haven't given it that much thought."

She turned to him. "How? I mean, why not? I've been a werewolf a couple months and it is all I think about. It's ten times harder to focus on school. I obsess. I feel like it's going to ruin my whole life."

"It might," Jules replied. "It's why Marissa left me."

He had met Marissa at the Culinary Institute of America. A brunette with captivating eyes, more welcoming (and more plump) than the French girls he'd met and more down-to-earth than most American girls. She had a playful laugh and a gift for desserts. When they graduated with their bachelors degrees, he'd convinced her to come to Paris with him and complete the program at Le Cordon Bleu. For nine months, they'd lived a total cliché: studying at the famous French cooking school, exploring Paris, perfecting Marissa's language skills, living together and sharing the same bed. She always smiled easily and when she wore her glasses, they often slipped down her soft and perfect nose.

He had proposed to her their last evening together, four years ago, after they had finished the program and he landed a job at a restaurant run by two older chefs where he adored their seafood-heavy menu. Marissa would return to the United States the next day, where she would start her tenure as a saucier in a prestigious fine dining establishment. He still remembered the ache that prompted him to propose: the thought of no more Marissa to talk to, no more delectable desserts dripping with cherry syrup, no more Marissa to touch. His heart oozed out of his chest. She accepted, but refused his offer to buy her a ring, as you can't wear a ring in a commercial kitchen.

But she hadn't known then.

"I told her I'd move to New York as soon as I could," Jules told Minette as they sat on his love seat.

"But you never did," she said.

"No," he replied, "because she came back to Paris to visit and..."

He had never told the story to anyone. He had swallowed it and kept it buried within, the impact of it fading over the years, but the pain could always be renewed in an instant. He would feel the familiar sucker punch of loss when he caught a brown-eyed girl looking at him in just the right way or when an unusual cake struck a familiar spot on his taste buds. Sometimes the misery hit simply because a woman on the street wore a dress that resembled something Marissa had once worn.

And now, after all these years, Jules was about to tell his little sister.

It had happened while jogging. Not a very French thing to do, but it helped Jules keep his adrenalin focused. Between lots of exercise and the custom-compounded Haldol-Ativan pills his father had prescribed, the wolf remained suppressed. Marissa had struggled to match his pace, she always did. Her participation meant more time to spend with him— as the lifestyle of student chefs did not allow much leisure. He had paused in front of Notre Dame, the cathedral's ornate towers extending into the dark night and the church's spotlights bleeding orange against the black clouds.

A whistle had penetrated the air, a sound addressed solely to him. He had glanced toward the statues on the church wall and the familiar, dark purple wisps. They had darted at Marissa, like insect fireworks around her head.

"What?" he had asked, recognizing the fairy energies as the gargoyles who normally toyed with him when he ran in this neighborhood at night.

"Wait," present-day Minette interrupted as he told the story. "Seriously? Tiny fairy gargoyles?"

"They were trying to get my attention," Jules explained.

"You need to write a book," Minette muttered.

"I told you this is a world unlike anything you ever imagined."

"I want to meet fairies."

You will," Jules said.

He continued his story, the same story he had replayed in his mind many times. He thought unloading the tale would provide a catharsis but in reality... He didn't want to face it. Ever.

On that perfect Paris night, a scream had filled the hollowness of the near-midnight hour. A body had barreled toward them, speeding straight from above. Marissa had blanched and then she froze, or maybe she didn't have a chance to move. She did not have Jules' razor-sharp senses and reflexes. A man had hurtled through the air, his winter coat flying behind him like a kite.

That's when, in one fierce motion, Jules had turned.

His bones creaked and extended. His jaw exploded and his nose bled. He had that familiar ache as the teeth shot through his gums. His body rippled with extra muscle. His thighs bulked to twice their size. His toes sprouted claws that burst from his shoes.

It all happened in seconds. As Jules recalled it, Marissa lost all color and her respirations grew shallow.

"Do I need to keep going?" he asked.

"Just talking about it," Minette said, "you've changed. Your tone. It's intense. And I can't explain it, but... when your eyes meet mine, my body absorbs your rage."

"I can stop," he said, his voice a raspy version of itself. "I saved her, but I also terrified her. To know is one thing... but to experience it..."

He rose and went toward the kitchen. Minette seized his wrist as he turned. He peered over his shoulder.

"Please keep going," she said.

"I need a glass of water."

He moved slowly— retrieving the glass, grabbing a bottle of Perrier from the fridge, unscrewing and pouring it. He sighed, sipped, and put the bottle back in the refrigerator. He returned to the love seat.

"Marissa screamed louder than the howling man falling from the sky," he continued.

Jules had leaped over Marissa's head and tackled the man mid-air, knocking him to the ground a few feet to the side of Marissa. She had drawn her arms over her face and stood there, shaking, as she crumpled to her knees. Jules curled over the man like he had an American football to his chest.

"Was he dead?" Minette asked.

Jules nodded as he massaged the glass of water.

"He fell with such speed. I couldn't slow the impact. It was more like I pushed him to the side. And Marissa melted down. She hasn't talked to me since. And Min, I swore I'd never tell anyone else. "

"But you have to," she said. "You can't keep secrets like that forever."

"Min, when you tell someone your secrets, you can't control who they tell."

"But Jules, you can't spend your whole life alone."

Silence fell between them. They looked at each other with that non-verbal bond that only siblings have. Her eyes read him, because he watched her shoulders and upper body shift in sadness, maybe even pity.

"You can't," Minette repeated as Jules parted his lips, about to tell her that maybe he could.

Jules exhaled.

"But Jules... what happened to you, as a wolf, in that moment?"

Jules turned to her. A new reality struck him. Not only did she know, but she understood. She had lived that bone-twisting transformation. Jules closed his eyes as the hair on his arms and back rose. Wolf memories could be vague, but he could never forget them. As he closed his eyes, an electricity filled his veins. This warmed his skin and made even the air brushing across it a heavy sensation.

"It was instinct," he said. "I had to protect my mate."

When he opened his eyes, the heat in his body and around him dissipated. The air cooled. His sensitivity dropped.

"And now you can change at-will?" Minette asked.

He nodded.

"And that medication Dad gave you?"

"It suppressed my body's reaction to stress, adrenaline and arousal," he said, "but I've learned better coping mechanisms."

"You have to teach me," she said.

"We should talk to Dad," he said.

"I told you," she replied, the anger building in her voice, "I won't be his experiment."

"Maybe you already are," he blurted out.

"That's what you think?" she retorted

"He started feeding me pills as soon as he suspected," Jules said. "And then Benji didn't have it. So that left you… and he knew you didn't have it. You're the girl. The carrier. What if he did… do something?"

"That's insane, Jules."

He stood up, shrugged, and returned his now empty water glass to the kitchen.

"Is it?" he asked.

She rose from the couch and paced the small living room, peering out the window and offering a slight smile to the Paris street below.

"How would we even find out?" she asked. "It's not like I can walk into a medical office and tell them I think my dad is performing medical experiments on me without my consent."

Jules gasped. "What if we could?"

Retrieving his flip phone from his pocket, Jules scrolled through the numbers. He wondered if he had Jacqueline Saint-Ebène's digits, and he did. But did he want to see her? And did he want to expose his sister to a military doctor? Could he trust her? And could she manage to navigate the system without putting them at risk?

"Jules?" his sister said.

"I know someone. She helped me get my medication. And she's the one who taught me I didn't need it."

"So she knows?" Minette asked.

Jules nodded.

"Didn't you just say you can't tell people your secrets?"

He glared at her. "Yeah, because she's a military doctor and I've seen Dog Soldiers."

They stared at each other in silence. That was the thing about siblings— you didn't have to say much to know exactly what the other is thinking. Jules knew his sister wanted to understand all of this, hated his contradictions, and wanted to strangle him for not knowing more about his own life as a werewolf.

Her engineering studies at Lafayette College suited her analytical brain. Her career path might lead her to build bridges or control municipal water flow. He, on the other hand, blended the structured and the free. His life in the hierarchy of the commercial kitchen included the creativity of combining new tastes and exciting dishes. He considered himself an artist, and as an artist, you had to be open to the experience versus the scientific details.

Maybe he should call Jacqueline, have her draw their blood or something, see how they compared. But asking her to do it meant a huge risk. Minette thought their father would see her as a lab rat. Would Jacqueline? Would the prospect of a second werewolf cause her to reveal their secret, if only accidentally? And then there's the fact that she worked for the military, and he had indeed seen Dog Soldiers.

"So, you're lecturing me because you told someone who you shouldn't have told?" Minette said.

Jules grumbled. "It's a long story."

"Maybe we should tell Dad," she said.

"You'll need your passport," Jules said.

"I meant call them," she said.

"But you need to get back into the United States eventually," he said. "And soon if you want to come with me to Chicago."

"So I need to call them," Minette replied. "But if I do…"

She didn't finish the sentence.

"Yes, Min?"

"We need to figure out everything we know, and what you can teach me. You relied on Dad as some sort of know-it-all for too long."

"Should we call Jacqueline?"

"Do we need a doctor?" she asked.

"I don't know what answers you are looking for," he said.

"Can we trust her?" Minette asked.

He shrugged. "I don't know."

CHAPTER FIVE

Jules had prepared coffee, strong. It swirled in the press like a bitter syrup, no light reflecting or passing through its grasp. It sat proudly on the counter, a clean mug and spoon beside it. The sight brought him back to last week, suddenly adrift in the volcanic desert landscape of East Africa, the hunger burning in his gut from the energy he expended as a werewolf.

Principal Doctor Jacqueline Saint-Ebène and her unit had built a temporary combat support hospital as a practice exercise. Despite a recent gunshot wound inflicted by Étienne, her superiors had handed her a bottle of opiates and told her to lead it. Jules didn't know all this at the time when he stumbled to her side. He merely found a dusty, exhausted military hospital leader jotting notes in her journal, the frayed ribbon attached to the spine flapping ever so slightly in the quiet air. Her pale, slender hands— dainty but steady— ripped open two rations of instant coffee and added them into one cup of hot water. And she drank it black, as happens during deployment. And she didn't even wince.

So, when the notorious Doc Saint arrived in his upper-level Parisian apartment, he presented her with steaming black coffee. Earlier this week, Jacqueline had left the military hospital Bouffard in Djibouti for Val-de-Grâce here in Paris. The coincidence, that all of them seemed to be forever floating between continents at the same time and ending up in the same place, bothered him in that way that premonitions felt dark. Jacqueline seemed happy to see him. Her posture gave him no signs that she didn't want to be near him. Her body temperature and scents matched what he expected of her.

"How's…"

Jules motioned to his own chest. Jacqueline gave a slight nod and a hint of a shoulder shrug.

"It hurts," she said. "But the wound looks clean and is healing well."

She gulped the coffee.

"Are you still taking painkill—"

"Oh no," she interrupted.

She stifled a small laugh that came out her nose.

"That was just to survive the weekend exercise," she said. "I'm too much of a thrill-seeker to stay on that kind of sauce. I'd be utterly fearless."

That certainly made sense to Jules. And explained how her body ended up draped across the bench in the bed of an army truck, his body diving against her with a depth and a violent need he'd never felt before, both naked and sweaty in the vivid sun… How he had ended up having the kind of sex he never considering having… the sensations of which, well, he never knew people did those things like that and enjoyed them because he was literally half animal which led him to believe only the wolf in him would want that.

Jacqueline smiled and accepted the coffee very unapologetically, sweeping into the tiny living room and sitting on the love seat.

"Cute, little place," she said.

That was one of those classic French comments— offer a compliment that you didn't really mean, with a hint of disdain, recognizing someone's achievements and failures in one judgmental phrase. Even on the couch, she maintained perfect posture. Her wavy, brown hair swayed ever-so-minutely below her chin as she made an effort to maintain eye contact between Jules, standing in the middle of the room, and Minette, slouched forward in anticipation on the chair near the window.

Her mind obviously had stayed in the present and she had no issue with their recent tryst. Except maybe for the devilish twist in the corner of her lips when she ran her eyes across him. But from what he'd seen, she unabashedly looked at everyone like that.

"So you want me to analyze your blood," Jacqueline said.

Already, her sharp gaze studied them.

"Well," Jules said, "I'm no doctor so I don't really know what would be prudent."

She continued drinking her coffee. As her the sleeve of her uniform jacket jiggled, Jules caught a glimpse of a bracelet near the hem of her blouse. It seemed uncharacteristically heavy for someone from a family of spoiled, upper class women.

"But you think I can find some test to determine what activated your sister's lycanthropy."

That snapped Jules from his obsession with Jacqueline's arm, and her fingers wound around the warm mug.

"We were hoping so," he said.

"Does it matter?" Jacqueline replied.

Jules flinched. Of course, it mattered. Answers always mattered. Jules turned to his sister, who looked blankly at him. Jacqueline gulped the thick coffee. The bracelet peeked out again, and he thought he saw a blinking light. Jacqueline followed his gaze.

"We're not looking for a way to reverse it, are we?" Jacqueline asked.

Minette drew closer. If she wanted to close the conversation any more, she'd need to move the chair.

"I didn't consider that," Minette responded.

"Neither did I," Jules said with hesitation.

"I need to know what you're looking for," she said crisply. "A test has to yield a result. And while I can easily tell you your blood type or your sodium levels or if your joints are healthy, that's not what you're asking me."

She paused. Her tone had sharpened. And from the way she relaxed her expression, Jules knew that she recognized her change in demeanor.

"I love a puzzle," she said sweetly. "And I love what human bodies can do and how I get to fix them. But I need to know what you are looking for. There's a difference between reaching understanding, managing symptoms, and dealing with something completely broken."

She had moved from analytical doctor to the empathetic listener. The shift in the tone of her voice had to come from years of bedside manner.

"Do you think you're broken?" she asked. "I need you to think about that."

Jacqueline set the coffee mug on the small table. Again, Jules got a glimpse of the bracelet. If he focused hard enough, he thought he could hear it pulse.

"It's a monitoring device," Jacqueline said tersely. "Please stop staring at it."

"Are you okay?" Minette asked with a sweet, concerned tone.

Jacqueline chuckled.

"It's a location monitoring device, not a medical one," she said after a pause. "I'm a naughty girl."

Jules picked up her empty mug and met her eyes, directly. With the mug in his left hand and blocking his sister's view with his body, Jules gestured with his right index finger between them.

"Because of what we——"

"Don't flatter yourself," Jacqueline interrupted. "You're just a footnote in a military training exercise. 'Unit rescued lost civilian, European male, treating for dehydration and returned to the city center.'"

Jules brought the mug to the kitchen sink.

"I can't even say it's because I rightfully intervened in a medical emergency involving a native girl, because the military doesn't really value morals over rules. In the end, it's about my possession of an unauthorized handgun, and getting shot with it. But this isn't about my military misadventures..." Jacqueline said. "It's about my unauthorized study of a hereditary, tetragametic chimera disorder that results in lycanthropy."

"Hereditary tetra-what chimera disorder?" Jules repeated as he stepped back into the room.

Jacqueline pulled her pocket-sized notebook out of her medical bag. The ratty brown journal had once been perfect, crisp leather but now was worn and scuffed. She opened it at the ribbon attached to the spine, flipping backwards toward the front of the book.

"You have notes on me?" Jules said.

"Not on you, per se," she answered. "I just happened to make notes about hypothetical DNA disorders."

Minette moved closer. "Is that safe?"

"Neither of you have answered my question. What are you looking for? Why did you come to me?"

Jules sat on the couch beside her, clasped his hands together and lowered his head.

"Ever since I... changed... for the first time, my dad treated me like something to be feared," he explained. "You didn't. I learned more about my body from you than I learned from my own experience."

"Okay," she said, motioning impatiently. "Keep going."

"I think he's trying to say that he believes you could help us understand without making me feel like the biggest freak in the room," Minette added.

"You are the biggest freak in the room," Jules said.

Jacqueline made some notes. "But that still doesn't tell me how I can help."

"Can you compare whatever we know about me to whatever we know about her," Jules said. "Girls are carriers, not werewolves. Did something mutate? Is she sick?"

Jacqueline leaned into the couch cushions.

"You want me to clandestinely perform genetic testing on the two of you?"

Jules shrugged. His hands stayed planted on his knees but his shoulders flared.

"The last person I had perform genetic testing for me, secretly, was your father."

Minette sighed. "What is the point of any of this?"

"Wait!" Jules exclaimed. "That's perfect. Send the samples to my father. Ask him to analyze them and send you the results. Don't tell him who the samples came from."

"Okay," Jacqueline said.

She set the notebook between herself and Jules on the love seat. Rummaging through her bag, she retrieved a needle and kept digging.

"I don't carry collection tubes for these kinds of tests on me," she said. "So I'll come back tomorrow."

Tomorrow sounded far away. But if she intended to send the samples to their father, nothing would come of this quickly. Jules wanted this over.

"Hey," Jacqueline said.

She placed her hand on his knee. Her warm hand rested on his leg. His heart rate jumped. He hoped nothing else would. She had the kindest, softest expression on her face; she looked at him like a friend, like someone who cared. He spent all these years thinking anyone who loved him would consider him a monster if they found out, but maybe he had it wrong.

"There are some tests I can run here," Jacqueline said. "Well, maybe not in your living room."

He wasn't sure if he liked her tendency to make everything into a joke.

"The logical place to start would be hormones," she said, and he wasn't sure she was talking to them. "Maybe I can snag some time for an fMRI. We definitely should meet at the hospital, as soon as I work out the details."

"Well, we need to get back to the States," Jules said, "as soon as we find Min's passport."

"There's so many things that haven't been resolved," Jacqueline said. It was the first time he heard sadness in her voice. "You're still looking for Étienne?"

Jules nodded. "Madame has traced him to Chicago."

Jacqueline turned to Minette. "This is all crazy."

Jacqueline rose from the couch and stepped behind it, sinking her fingers into her hair on both sides of her head and combing through the wavy brunette locks. She walked toward the kitchen.

"Do you ever ponder the bigger picture? Not even six months ago— Adelaide Pitney was a supermodel and my brother-in-law's muse. You..."

She stopped at the arm of the couch by Jules.

"...were cooking here in Paris. And you..."

She reached toward Minette.

"... well, I'm guessing you weren't a werewolf. And I was just a combat surgeon who didn't always follow orders. Something bigger is happening."

"The creative forces of the universe are in upheaval," Jules said.

"Melodramatic much?" Minette responded.

"Are they supposed to be?" Jacqueline asked. "Did Adelaide unleash something? Or was she part of the natural order?"

Jules peered at her, this intelligent yet feisty woman. He looked to the floor, hiding his reddening cheeks. Jacqueline and Minette had given 'the big picture' way more thought than he ever had. They both faced this supernatural curse, and he... ran away. He did what he was expected to do and kept to himself.

"I don't know," he said.

"What if..." Jacqueline continued as her pacing resumed, "... what if this whole situation has gotten derailed? What if your sister isn't supposed to be a werewolf? What if recent events caused a need for a female wolf? How is this connected to Étienne?"

"Maybe it's not," Jules said.

Minette leaned against the television stand.

"It has to be," Jacqueline said. "Étienne was touched by a god-power in the Ogaden, and has attracted the supernatural since, right?"

"You mean Neferkaba," Jules said. "Wait... Attracted the supernatural... So, when he went blind, that wasn't his first encounter with Neferkaba was it?"

"No. The running theory is that Neferkaba caused that accident in the Ogaden that put Étienne in that coma. And now, we suddenly have witch-girl

Adelaide helping my sister get pregnant," Jacqueline said while pacing. "And around the same time, a former flame of Étienne turns up pregnant. But you were recently charged with protecting one offspring, who hasn't been born yet. So Adelaide should not be part of this."

"I'm not sure I follow," Jules said.

"I know I don't," Minette said.

Jacqueline explained her logic: Sélène LeBlocque, the main nurse who treated Étienne after he almost drowned in Lake Assal and sustained a head injury during his conscripted service, found herself in Val-de-Grâce after an IUD expulsion. Jacqueline discovered that Sélène was pregnant despite no sexual contact. The investigation revealed that Étienne had fathered the fetus, even though Étienne had last seen her in 1978. Étienne had interacted with this Spirit Guardian force, which had saved his life, but somehow twisted the notions of reproduction and time.

"Okay," Jules agreed.

But did that bring them any closer to understanding what was happening?

Jacqueline continued breaking down the past. Étienne had noticed Adelaide Pitney at the airport in Chicago in 1990. Everyone in the Saint-Ebène family could repeat the story. This twelve-year-old girl with the voluminous strawberry blonde hair and blue eyes as deep and shining as lapis lazuli inspired and launched his first collection of ready-to-wear clothes. And unbeknownst to her, at least until near the end, Adelaide possessed a feminine water magick passed down from Celtic ancestors centuries earlier. She inadvertently used this magick to allow Basilie to birth a child.

"Again, I know that," Jules said.

The familiar sourness filled his mouth, as Jules never liked Adelaide. Unlike the others— perhaps because he and Adelaide were from the same generation— he was never taken in by her beauty. She came off as shallow, disorganized and out-of-touch.

"I didn't know any of that," Minette said. "And none of it makes sense."

"It doesn't," Jacqueline agreed. "Not in what we believe is reality. But what if... Adelaide made a mistake when she gave Basilie the ability to have a baby, and that one mistake led to all of this. That Adelaide's interference also threatens to transfer Sélène's baby to Kait, the former water guardian, and Étienne's reactions to these events, and maybe our own, keep making everything more complicated and screwed up."

"So you are saying Sélène's baby has a purpose that has been in motion since 1978," Jules summarized, "and that everything else is random human folly?"

"Maybe," Jacqueline said.

"What about me?" Minette said.

"If Adelaide bent the rules, so to speak, as to what should happen and how, maybe that changed the rules in other realms, like with hereditary werewolf disorders," Jacqueline surmised.

Jacqueline retrieved her notebook and scribbled within it, not stopping until she had filled several pages. Jules and Minette looked quizzically at one another.

"So, we find Kait, and we find Étienne, and hopefully Sélène will have her baby?" Jules asked. "But there's also the issue of the missing spirit guardian."

Jacqueline looked up from her notes.

"This Spirit Guardian was depicted to me as the god of the gods, so to speak. How can she go missing?"

"I don't know how it works." Jules shrugged. "I serve Kait. If she asks me to do something, I do it."

"What if you don't?" Jacqueline asked.

"Kait... was a monster. I found that out the hard way."

He had no desire to recount Kait's initial visits to his childhood home where she'd drag him out of bed, threatening to get a choke chain and a cattle prod.

"Something about Adelaide changed her," he told them, "or maybe when she slept with Étienne the magick that made her pregnant returned her to her natural mind."

Jacqueline made more notes. Minette stretched, extending her long, lanky limbs from the chair, and paced the room. Minette's eyes surveyed the different accents in the room: the coffee table he used as a TV stand, the small bookcase filled with cookbooks, the loveseat, and the jar of peanut butter M&Ms. She walked toward the M&Ms.

"I wouldn't," Jules told her. "They have got to be six months old."

She raised her eyebrows, reached for the jar, grabbed a handful and shoved them into her mouth.

"Taste fine," she said.

"We have to get to Chicago," Jules reiterated. "Min, call Benji and see if he can go to Mom and Dad's and get your passport."

"Okay," she said.

Jules glared at her.

"Now?" she asked.

"Yeah," he snapped. "You can do it from my bedroom."

She pointed with her thumb over her shoulder as the narrow hall that led to the bedroom and bathroom was behind her.

"I can go call our brother from your bedroom."

"Yes," Jules insisted.

He wanted to talk to Jacqueline alone.

"This is the worst trip to Paris ever," she said as she turned.

She reluctantly trudged down the hall. Jules waited until he heard the bedroom door close.

"Did Madame tell you?" Jules asked. "About why Étienne is in Chicago?"

Jacqueline flipped the pages in her notebook back two or three sheets. He thought he recognized the word "delusional" among the chaos of her doctor's handwriting.

"Yes," she said. "My sister thinks Adelaide is alive."

She tapped the word with her pen.

CHAPTER SIX

Their passports were in transit from what seemed like opposite corners of the world. Jacqueline had drawn their blood, swapping out tube upon tube and capping them with various colored lids.

"I think a thyroid panel and DHEA may give us some interesting comparisons," she said when she finished the last set of tubes. "It will give us some different views of your hormones."

She said she would slip into the hospital's clinical lab and attempt to perform the tests herself.

Now, they were waiting for the fMRI. Minette sat beside him in a dark, sterile hallway, with gritty, speckled beige tiles and an off-color light blue wall with a random tan chair rail. The chairs themselves were a row of four industrial, square vinyl-cushion-on-metal-frame relics from maybe the 1950s, way before his time. Jacqueline had asked them both to dress "smartly" so he had dug his dress shoes from the closet, a pinstripe shirt and navy blue slacks (which Étienne would have insisted they have a crease down the leg). Minette still only had the black jeans she bought so he had given her some money to buy something. She opted for a mild floral print criss-crossy dress that she explained was "a faux wrap." Before they entered the hallway, Jacqueline handed Jules a stethoscope and Minette a clipboard.

"You are med students," she explained. "And you are shadowing me. A research project on civilian versus military care."

Jacqueline brought him into a changing room. At her direction, Jules stripped and put on a gown. Jacqueline collected him and he entered the smooth mouth of the machine. Jacqueline said he had to be the control. She slid a massive plastic cage over his head and used a pillow and mirror so he could view a small screen. The earphones muffled the beeping of the machine somewhat, but he struggled to stay calm and still through her directions: listen to words (somehow she had learned the name of his fiancée, probably thanks to Minette), repeat phrases, and pinch his fingers. Only his head went into the machine, but by the end of the test, every muscle in his body rippled with stiffness and annoyance.

When Jacqueline released him, she didn't make eye contact. Nervous energy hovered around her, it struck him more as a smell than a visual, similar to the oily scent of asphalt rising from the street on a hot and humid day.

"What did you see?" he asked.

Jacqueline moved in a careful, methodical way. Her lips tightened in a way unnatural for her.

"Jacqueline, you're not just a doctor to me," he reminded her. "We're not friends, I know, but we have a bond now."

He sat up from the sled of the machine.

"I put that on my list of reasons not to sleep with another werewolf," she said.

"So what did you see? You're afraid now. I can smell it."

She exhaled. It was her way of willing her body to relax. It failed.

"I'm not afraid of you," she said. She smiled weakly. "I'm afraid of what would happen if these scans ended up in the wrong hands. Let's get your sister in here and we'll talk later."

Minette, in her flimsy hospital gown, stood in the doorway. Jules rose from the machine and intentionally grazed her fingers with his as he walked past her to the changing area. He paused for a second. She tentatively moved toward the device.

"Min," he called quietly.

She turned.

"None of this is a big deal," he said. "I'm going to take care of you."

"I'm not terminally ill," she replied.

But he saw it— what he wanted to see— the slight shift in her body language, softening of her posture that told him she wasn't nervous. Not anymore. Jacqueline reiterated the directions to Minette. Jules got dressed. While waiting for his sister and Jacqueline, he tucked the stethoscope into his ears and pressed it against his own chest. Almost instantly, he ripped out the earpieces. The whooshing and thumping reverberated with an intensity that made his eardrums shake. The pain erupting from deep in his head and tumbling out his ear canal made him brace his skull.

What did they expect to find? Jules wondered if maybe the search for answers would only lead to more questions. His whole lived experience with this werewolf shit had been some surreal hijacking of what he thought was reality. And now Min. But between the two of them, they had to sniff out Étienne and put to rest this idea that Adelaide was alive. The funeral and the subsequent ordeal with her ghost haunting and then her possession of Étienne had drained everyone. It had gotten them involved with a madman, a killer who wanted first Adelaide's latent magick and then her very spirit.

Jules had failed in his obligation to protect Étienne and Basilie d'Amille from the supernatural forces that had entered their sphere. Adelaide had brought darkness upon them in her shallow ignorance and hedonism. Without her missteps, Étienne would be here. Basilie would have not had a stroke. And he wouldn't have traversed the rocky Horn of Africa desert and slept with the cute army doctor giving his sister an fMRI right now.

And maybe Minette would be safe in her dorm room or underage drinking in Mexico like a normal American college student on spring break.

And maybe without the werewolf gene he would be happily married to Marissa.

Lost in thought, Jules didn't notice Jacqueline and Minette approaching until they stood normal-people-would-notice distance from him. Minette was already in her dress. Jacqueline had a distant but analytical expression on her face. Both had familiar feminine scents. And he sensed that one of them would start their menstrual cycle soon. He had twisted the stethoscope, wringing it like a damp rag.

"Jules, you okay?" Minette asked.

Jules chuckled. He slowly rose and draped the stethoscope over his shoulders.

"Yeah," he said. "I'm just so sorry you have to deal with this, Min."

She suddenly hugged him. Footsteps clattered somewhere nearby. If his ears could be trusted, other people would be in the corridor soon.

"It's not your fault," she said, clinging to him tightly. "Blame our parents."

Jacqueline surveyed the hall. She heard it now.

"Let's head to my office," she said.

Her office occupied the corner of one of the patient wards of the hospital, a converted mini-break room with a small round table, one window, a counter, a cupboard, a hand-washing sink and a coffee pot. Four hard plastic chairs surrounded the table. Two more flanked the window. A laptop anchored a pile of what Jules assumed were patient charts and random papers on one side of the table.

"I'm a medical nomad," Jacqueline said as her arm motioned for them to sit. "Coffee?"

Jacqueline opened the cupboard and pulled down coffee mugs. Two were plain, the type that might have been borrowed from the hospital kitchen, but one had some elaborate paragraph about the special call and heart of a nurse. Jacqueline poured herself a coffee, drinking it black while leaning against the counter.

"You drink a lot of coffee," Jules observed.

"I have to," she said. "There are certain bad habits everyone picks up in the military. Overconsumption of coffee is one. Until recently, smoking was the other. The career guys lament the end of cigarettes and wine in field rations."

Minette walked across the room and poured herself coffee.

"So what was the point of the scans?" she asked.

"They allow me to compare your brain patterns, to a normal person and to each other," she said. "If I didn't know you, I would think you had a psychiatric condition like schizophrenia or that you were psychopaths."

Minette's face grimaced when Jacqueline said that. It made sense to Jules. The idea of having an animal in your DNA inherently meant you might not fit the traditional healthy psychological profile. And a wolf didn't care about human norms. They had their own society and structure.

"Even without running the blood tests," Jacqueline continued, pulling Jules from his contemplation. "I can see that the two of you have similar brains and that confirms that she is adapting to the condition, but we don't know why."

"Similar," Jules repeated, "but not the same."

"No two brains are the same," Jacqueline said. "You both have amygdala activity that surpasses the average person, and Jules yours is much more controlled than Minette's."

"What does that mean?" Jules asked.

"I had psych last year," Minette said. "The amygdala controls anxiety and fear."

Smarty-pants, Jules scoffed internally.

"It's the part of the brain that looks for danger and controls your responses," Jacqueline said. "And both your brains respond to everything as fast as the machine can register it. My anecdotal observation is that as those reactions heighten, the rational parts of your brain deactivate."

"Wait... does that mean we can't think?" Minette said.

"I can vouch for that," Jules said. "All that is left is instinct."

"If you wanted to know if what was happening to Minette is real," Jacqueline said. "The answer is yes. Her brain is transforming. How the chimera DNA implants on her X chromosomes, I don't know. That's a question you'll have to ask your parents."

Awkward silence consumed the room.

"They don't know, Jacqueline," Jules said. "No one knows. This is all a guessing game."

"I could send a psychiatrist friend your results," Jacqueline said, "if you want more insight."

"Maybe someday," Jules said.

She handed him a compact disc in a plain jewel case.

"This is the only copy," Jacqueline said. "Someday you may want your dad to have it."

"Thanks," Jules said.

"I'll have a full report soon," she said.

CHAPTER SEVEN

Before they could make arrangements to fly to Chicago, Jules had to stop by the Chez d'Amille Paris office for the passports. Laurentine, the receptionist of sorts, had received his from DHL. Benji had FedExed Minette's passport from California. The covert passport retrieval operation sent Benji to their parents' house for dinner, where he then could sneak the document from Minette's room.

Benji hadn't asked many questions, and for that Jules thanked the gods, whoever or whatever they may be. Benji had started with the classic "How did she get to Paris without her passport?" but Jules had replied with a "Not now." Benji had nabbed the passport and reported that he had sent it to them at the Paris office.

Chez d'Amille's headquarters had a broad front stair and a heavy wooden door that didn't quite match the Hausmannized, nineteenth-century city the world recognized. The rest of the building fit the aesthetic of the surrounding buildings, but the door and stairwell transported Jules to brownstones in Brooklyn.

Upon entrance, Laurentine greeted Jules with a sly French, half-smile and a cock of her head, playfully shifting the weight of her messy but precisely-styled Audrey Tautou-lookalike, almost-chin length bob. A perfect red lip, a red and black silk scarf at her neck, a crisp white blouse and a tailored pencil skirt completed her ensemble. As the person at the door, Laurentine had the most pressure to always be put together. And every time he saw her, Jules admired her efforts and thought she enjoyed her role. *She offered Jules les bises.* He returned them.

"So this is your sister, Margot-Antoinette," Laurentine said. "We have a surprise for her."

Laurentine gestured toward the showroom, an open salon with shining hardwood floors, mirrors, and long vertical windows. To Jules, the simplicity of it seemed like a classy ballet studio. Jules led his sister deeper into the room. Minette moved slowly. Her eyes glittered with something akin to awe or maybe confusion. She had braided her hair this morning, one twist on either side of her head. It gave her a childlike glow.

Laurentine followed them into the room, her heels reverberating against the floor and flashing their trendy red soles. Étienne loved shoes. He often gifted them to his staff. Jules himself had a luxurious pair of Salvatore Ferragamo loafers in black leather. He rarely wore them, as expensive Italian shoes and commercial kitchens do not mesh well, nor do the streets of Manhattan lend themselves toward keeping shoes clean.

Laurentine touched Minette gently on the elbow and directed her to the ornate, metal bench with a peacock in its iron work, its tail reaching toward whoever sat with him. Minette sat. Laurentine then gracefully moved to a buffet between the two entry doors and retrieved an already opened, flat, cardboard envelope emblazoned with stickers from the overnight carrier.

Laurentine handed it to Jules. When he opened the flap, he found the passports.

"What's going on?" he asked. "This is all we need."

"We have a surprise," Laurentine announced. "I will get you water. With gas or without?"

"With," he replied.

Jules glanced to Minette. Chez d'Amille functioned on a trademark (and ridiculous) blend of surprise and extravagance. Laurentine disappeared and reappeared with three slender glasses and a one liter bottle of Perrier. Minette sat quietly on the bench, her eyes fixed on Jules. Suddenly, Laurentine had macarons on a platter. Minette accepted a small plate of several pastel cookies and an embroidered napkin.

As Minette lifted the sweet confection toward her lips, a macaron in a vivid yellow, Jules heard a rustle from the far end of the room. The only door from that side led to an oversized storage closet, where Étienne primarily stored and organized his dress forms of his most common clients. Laurentine arranged glasses of water and the remaining macarons on a small round table beside the bench, not noticing what Jules had. Minette also did not hear. He wondered if his supernatural hearing had depicted something the human ear could not.

With minimal disturbance to the room around him, Jules turned toward the odd closet. With the women in his peripheral vision and his neck hairs raised like the hackles of a dog, Jules carefully crept without making a single sound, moving toward the noise. A stifled cough, like someone trying to hold their breath and failing, emanated from behind the closed door. Jules extended his hand toward the doorknob, sure there was a man inside, and from the feel and smell of it, it wasn't one of the men from the atelier.

Jules jerked open the door. From inside the closet, amid the organized shadows of women's bodies, a man jumped. He stood next to a plain, black, carry-on suitcase. When the light filled the entry of the storage room, the man instinctively threw himself behind the tallest dress form not tucked onto a shelf. Like Minette and Jules, he had thick dark brown hair but his was short with just a scoop of bangs across his forehead. He stood two inches shorter that Jules, but had the same brown eyes and the same slender nose. But unlike Jules, who stared at the twenty-something with a tense expression and a body coursing with adrenaline, when the 'intruder' recognized him, his broad mouth turned upward into a gregarious smile.

"Benji," Jules muttered.

Benji circled the muslin-covered female torso on a stick and released a hearty laugh as he emerged into the main showroom. The darkness under his eyes and the hint of wrinkles in his fitted, v-neck t-shirt suggested he might have been traveling for a while.

"So this is the surprise?" Jules asked no one in particular as he retrieved his older brother's suitcase and closed the closet door.

"Benji!" she screamed.

Minette ran across the room and leapt into his arms. He caught her, wrapping her in a tight hug. He spun her so her feet lifted from the ground.

"That's why you didn't ask questions," Jules said.

Benji lowered Minette to the floor and patted his hands on his crisp dark jeans.

"I decided I'd see for myself what trouble the two of you are in," he said.

"We're not in trouble," Jules grumbled.

"Minette arrived in Paris without a passport," Benji reminded them.

Jules went for a glass of water from the table. Laurentine pressed close to him.

"That is not *our* surprise," she said.

Once again, Jules tensed. "No?"

Laurentine smirked. The sigh Jules so badly wanted to expel slipped slowly out his nose. Nothing at Chez d'Amille occurred without fanfare and excess, and Jules so badly wanted some peaceful discretion.

"How did you afford a last-minute ticket to Paris?" Jules asked Benji, not ready to deal with Laurentine.

Laurentine maneuvered toward the second entry, the one that led to the workrooms.

"Really, Jules? You don't think I can arrange a flight for myself?" Benji replied.

Jules shifted his body weight away from Benji.

"Just tell me you didn't tell Mom and Dad," Jules said.

"I didn't." Benji rolled his eyes. "I have a credit card, Jules."

"Well, you flew all this way just to turn around and fly to Chicago hopefully tomorrow."

"Chicago?" Benji repeated. "Well, one night in Paris is something. And I don't think I've ever been to Chicago—"

Laurentine eased herself from the room, leaving them to their confections and Perrier. His siblings chattered and enjoyed the cookies. Jules could not. It's not that he didn't like macarons— he did, unless he had to make them. Those little almond flour bastards and their moody meringues and the notion that every flavor had to have a precise color to label it... No, Jules was not a pastry chef. The macarons were always Marissa's domain.

Despite his ire for the iconic and pretentious sandwich cookie (which might also explain why Oreos achieved popularity in France), a familiar scent distracted Jules from the reunification party. Men's cologne, heavy on the citrus notes. Then, he tracked a familiar walk as it approached them. Before Jules had fully lowered his defenses, as his brain had not spread the message to his protective wolf self, Didier entered the room in his artful yet disapproving stance. In the showroom, he exuded confidence, a welcome change after his frazzled companion role in the heat of Djibouti. Here in his element, Didier wore his cream-colored lab coat like all of the sewing staff, with a pin cushion on his left wrist.

Ateliers ran similarly to commercial kitchens. A lot of barking, a lot of orders and a lot of rank. Here, Didier was Étienne's second-in-command and with Étienne missing this left him completely in charge. Didier had yet to shave. He had to be straight off the plane. The stubble on his face grew thicker near his chin. His hair seemed a little mussed, and Jules didn't know him well enough to know if that were intentional or a sign that he needed a haircut.

Seeing him here meant he had given up hope that Étienne was in Djibouti. Didier had, however, found fresh clothes since East Africa, his dark indigo, skinny jeans clung to his legs with a crisply upturned cuff, not too exaggerated, just a few centimeters to reveal his dark socks with white polka dots. His brown eyes carried the heaviness of their recent adventures.

"Hey Didier," Jules said. "I didn't expect to see you in Paris."

"Someone has to run the business," he replied. "Basilie made that quite clear."

So did he prefer to stay in Africa? Did she order him back? More people and wheels clattered in the hall. Two more of Étienne's staff members in lab coats pushed a fairly empty clothing rack into the room. As a staffer of the New York office, Jules didn't recognize the women. And as Jules scanned the rack, he didn't recognize the clothes either. They seemed muted by Chez d'Amille's usual standards. Jules didn't know quite how to pinpoint the feeling. When Étienne presented clothing, he preferred luxurious fabrics and ostentatious details. These clothes... would not seem out of place in an American shopping mall.

Maybe that was the point, Jules considered.

"Thank you, Odile, Nathalie, " Didier said.

The women quickly retreated. One had customized her jacket with ruffles on the back. Cute. The second had a smock that accented her waist unlike the shapeless drape on the other staff.

"I have assembled a trousseau for Mademoiselle," Didier said. "Basilie said she was flying you to Chicago, and asked me to make sure you had everything you need."

"Clothes?" Minette chirped.

"Yes, miss," Didier replied. "I assumed your sizes were similar to your brother, but feminine. And the staff has assembled these."

Didier gestured with an open arm to the rack. He offered no enthusiasm in the gesture, just statement of fact.

"And I now see the three of you share a body type," he said.

Minette walked slowly to it. She turned back to Jules and Benji.

"This is so weird," she said.

Jules nodded. Benji shrugged.

"We did what we could, on short notice," Didier said. "Most of them are Adelaide's ready-to-wear designs. You are... young... after all."

Didier said the word young as if it were a disease. After his dramatic delivery, Didier exited. The revelation that the clothes came from Adelaide's "Superstition" collection explained the bare-bones nature of the rack, and how the team could assemble the pieces so quickly. Around here, no one assembled a trousseau overnight.

Minette pushed hangers from one side of the rack to the other but didn't make a sound. She paused, gazed over her shoulder to her brothers, and looked again to the wardrobe presented to her.

"These are all my size," she said staidly. "How..."

"They just know," Jules said. "It's creepy."

Jules joined Benji on the bench. Benji patted his shoulder and pulled him into a half-hug.

"I've missed you, man," Benji said.

"This isn't how I imagined a reunion," Jules said.

Minette lifted a pink and white gingham sundress from the rack. She raised her arms over her head and whipped her sweater upward. She started to roll it off her arms, but froze.

"You're our sister," Jules told her.

"We're not looking," Benji added.

The sweater, the one she bought here in Paris, fell to the floor. The sleeveless dress went down her body and over her leggings— the same leggings she had on when she had traveled to Djibouti via a magickal wormhole. She gave a spin once the dress fell into position, and Jules, for the first time in years, saw his sister as the innocent, little girl he used to walk home from elementary school. He credited the braids for the nostalgia. And so it went. Minette piled the clothes she wanted over the bar on the top of the rack while she carefully returned the rejected items to the hanger.

Benji prattled on about his life in California, their parents and his latest surfing achievements. Benji spread his arm across the back of the bench and his knees before him. He projected his voice into the room without a care. Jules leaned forward and clasped his hands against his knees.

"Benji," Jules said. "Do you have any idea what is happening here?"

"Yeah, bro," Benji said. "Not a clue."

Minette had assembled a pile of three spring dresses; a pair of salmon-colored, high-waisted pinstripe pants with big white buttons decorating pockets facing the hips; a stormy sky, gray vest; a couple of cropped tops, one in white and one in a yellow buttercream; a turquoise flowing skirt with a tiny white paisley pattern, and a pair of tailored yet baggy pants in fuchsia.

"Benji," Jules said. "Min's wolf DNA activated."

"What?" Benji exclaimed.

Minette gulped her water, wincing, as if she had forgotten it was carbonated.

"Jules!" Minette snapped. "That wasn't your news to share."

Minette spun toward the door and crossed her arms.

"Are you serious?" Benji leapt to his feet. "So I'm the reject?"

Benji waved his arms in the air.

"Both of you have it. And I don't," Benji ranted.

"Have it?" Minette repeated in disgust.

Minette turned toward her oldest brother and whipped her index finger toward his nose. Jules rose and walked toward them.

"Guys—"

"You have no idea," Minette snapped. "Dad said this is impossible. And you want to make it about you?"

"Hello?" Benji replied. "I'm the first born."

"Guys—"

"And?" Minette replied. "It's not like this is an inheritance."

"But Dad wanted me to have it!" Benji exclaimed.

Jules sighed. He pushed himself between his siblings. He faced Benji.

"Dad wanted you to have it?" Jules said back to him. "Listen to yourself."

Benji's face got squinty.

"This isn't a college fund or... a fancy car," Jules said. "It's painful and unpredictable and comes with commitment and responsibility you can't understand. And Dad said it couldn't happen to a girl."

"Whatever," Benji said as he walked to the window.

"Benji," Jules said. "We're not children. We need to work together. We need to get Minette through this. And I have to find Étienne d'Amille."

CHAPTER EIGHT

None of them had ever visited Chicago, but Jules had read about the city and studied its culinary contributions to American culture. While working at the Culinary Institute, Jules scrutinized the regional cuisine of the United States. He pondered what he might eat as a vegetarian in the Windy City. His siblings had other concerns while approaching Étienne's Falcon jet, now sweetly wrapped in the silver Chez d'mille logo.

They boarded, receiving a greeting from Captain Luc. Minette froze in the doorway of the plane as if she had never flown before. She surveyed the beige leather seats and tiny tables and turned to her brothers.

"This ain't Delta," Benji remarked.

That's all it took to destroy the magic of the moment, Jules no longer felt like they were spoiled business travelers. Instead, they were clueless children bumbling through a private plane unable to decide on their seats.

"No," Jules said. "It is not."

Minter looked so posh in her plain, white cropped t-shirt with the high-waisted, bold pink pants from the atelier, and Jules had added to the ensemble by buying her a layered, gold chain. She had pulled her hair up, which gave her an older, more sophisticated look. Finally, she selected a chair in the middle of the plane. Benji sat beside her.

"The whole damn plane and you have to sit next to me?" she said.

Benji moved to the seat across the aisle.

"Better?" he asked.

Jules went two rows beyond them where he opened a small cabinet stuffed with liquor bottles: the tall, the stout, the pale, the robust, clear to dark caramel in glass that might be see-through or might be luscious green, or in the case of Chartreuse, the contents itself might be a vivacious glowing lime. Jules grabbed a glass. Upon opening the ice bucket and finding it fully stocked, he dropped a few cubes into the glass before pouring himself a hearty portion of VSOP brandy. With the drink in one hand, he gently massaged his forehead with the other.

Eight hours. Small private plane. No staff other than Captain Luc and his co-pilot. Hopefully his siblings would sleep.

"There's booze on this plane?" Benji exclaimed. "Is there food?"

"I packed sandwiches. Ham and butter on baguette," Jules replied.

Captain Luc's eyes went straight to Jules. The pilot cleared his throat.

"Are we ready, sir?" he asked.

Jules merely nodded. Captain Luc returned the gesture before he disappeared into the cockpit. In a few minutes the plane would initiate takeoff procedure. Jules sipped his brandy, wondering when, how and if everything would eventually make sense.

Benji still resented the fact that Minette had activated as a wolf and he had not. Madame d'Amille remained confident that Étienne would be at the Peninsula Hotel in Chicago with Adelaide. Jules hoped Madame was wrong, at least about Adelaide. Jules hoped he would find Étienne and Kait. Maybe Kait, the former water guardian and his supernatural boss, had convinced Étienne to help her, possibly because of their baby, the baby that Jacqueline had confirmed that Kait was Étienne's.

And even if they dealt with all that, they also had to determine what had happened to Neferkaba, the 'spirit' who supervised the elemental guardians. Jules prayed that it did not involve Adelaide Pitney.

Because Adelaide Pitney was dead.

And regardless of Adelaide's life status, Jules had to figure out why Minette—his sister, a female— had transformed successfully into a wolf and joined him as a protector of the guardians. Even if he ignored the genetic guidelines his father had set forth as the parameters of the inherited lycanthropy disorder, Jules couldn't quite accept that out of four sacred elements and four guardians that monitored the use of their power, that he and his sister served as werewolf protectors for half of them.

The plane started to roll from the gate. Spurred on by the realization that treats might lie within the compartments of the plane, Benji opened and closed every cabinet within reach of his seat.

Glancing to the brandy bottle, Jules grabbed it and migrated to the chair by the bathroom, the same one he had occupied when Étienne and Basilie had flown their whole crew to Paris a month ago. Before that flight, the plane had been commandeered by the French military police. Jules buckled himself into his seat and slipped his left hand into his pocket, caressing the meager supply of custom-compounded pills his father had ordered for him.

Sweat gathered on his forehead. The hairs on his neck bristled. Jules hated to fly. He put the brandy in the empty seat beside him. Minette and Benji chattered, but Jules closed his eyes and absorbed the rhythmic hum of the grounded jet. The plane rolled forward. Jules gripped his armrests. His muscles rippled up toward his skull. It felt like sinewy fingers threatening to strangle his brain.

And since he was a werewolf, he didn't know if the sensation was real. His body parts really might be migrating under his skin.

The plane pivoted. Jules opened his eyes and saw the edge of the runway out the porthole-style window. He slammed the shade down. His siblings hushed.

"Jules?" Minette said softly.

"Not now, Min," he returned.

The plane hurled itself across the tarmac. The nose lifted. Jules let the forces of gravity press him into his seat. The rear of the plane left the ground. The churning started in Jules' stomach. He unbuckled his seatbelt— despite the fact that the plane was climbing— and sailed toward the small lavatory. The brandy he had consumed made a return trip into the airplane toilet as Jules folded his tall, lanky body to the floor.

Jules pulled himself up, splashed water on his face, and returned to the cabin. He grabbed a bottle of water, chugging the contents. He slowly exhaled. The plane had reached cruising altitude. His sinuses pulsed with the artificial pressure in the plane. He took another deep breath and another exaggerated exhale before turning to Minette and Benji.

That's when he noticed that Benji had no color in his skin. His eyes had expanded into black coins and it seemed that he had lost his capacity to blink. His mouth hung open as if wanted to speak, his tongue pressed to the back of his front teeth. His attention focused on Minette.

Minette trembled with full-body vibrations. Jules dropped the water bottle. Jules ran to his sister's seat, retrieved the orange bottle from his pocket, popped the lid, and shoved two of the pills into her mouth. He stared, transfixed, perhaps even more than his brother, as her skin danced what Jules could only describe as independently across her face and down her arms. Jules' chest tightened. Now was not the time to discover that his sister also had issues with flying.

"What... why...." Benji stammered.

Her skin kept moving. Her body stiffened and straightened. Her skull elongated. Jules kept breathing, fighting his own body's urge to hyperventilate. And then... she relaxed. Her skin settled. Her face molded into its normal lines. Tears gathered in her eyes. Her hands trembled. Jules grabbed another bottle of water, unscrewed the cap, and handed it to her. She sipped it slowly.

"I... what... just..."

"Must be a werewolf thing," Jules interrupted. "I have always hated to fly. Except maybe it wasn't me—"

"What did you give me?"

"The pills Dad gave me," Jules explained. "Jacqueline told me it's a pretty strong sedative and a high-dose anti-psychotic. Dad had me taking them daily."

"I feel hollow," she said.

"The meds will do that," Jules said. "You'll feel rubbery for an hour or so."

"You lived like this?" she asked.

Heaviness overcame Jules.

"Dad had me really medicated. I just stopped them a few weeks ago," he said.

"I don't understand," Benji finally blurted. "What was that?"

"Her body started to shift into its wolf form," Jules said.

"Why?" Benji asked.

"I don't know," Jules replied. "I thought it was just me. My fear of flying. But maybe the wolf-part feels threatened by the notion of being in the air. Or the pressurized cabin triggers something."

Minette cried silently, sipping her water.

"I hate this," she said.

"It sucks," Jules said, "but you adapt."

Jules wrapped her hand in his.

"Get some sleep," Jules instructed.

"You can't just act like nothing happened," Benji said.

"I'm not," Jules replied.

"She's upset," Benji said.

"What do you want me to do?" Jules said, waving his arms in exasperation like a bird trying to lift off.

"This makes no sense," Benji said.

"I know," Jules said with sass dripping in the phrase. Sometimes his brother brought out the teenager in him. "We're not kids anymore, Benji. You're almost thirty. I've been living with this for a decade and I still don't know anything useful."

Jules fell into a nearby seat. The weight of trying to shield his sister from the changes in her life, his own discomfort with the airplane and his brother's ignorance all pulled on him.

"At least she isn't alone," Jules said.

He forced himself upright just enough to open the overhead compartments with the cozy blankets, pulling down three and tossing one at each sibling before layering his over his own body. Minette curled into hers in an attempt to get comfortable. Benji stood there, in the aisle, the blanket drooping. He looked at Jules with this lost expression as if he didn't know what to expect on a transatlantic flight or as if Jules had withheld information.

"But Jules—"

"Benji," Jules snapped. "I need some rest."

CHAPTER NINE

While technically luxurious and soft, the leather of the seats on the aircraft crinkled as Jules shifted his weight, adding to the constricting vibe within the metal tube with clanging engines and recirculated air. He planted his hands firmly on the shiny wooden accents of the chair's arms, ignored his siblings, and pretended he didn't hear the myriad gurgles and grinds of the opulent private jet from a company named after a bird.

If the noise came from waves, it would be okay. If he could hear the ocean below them, or feel the ocean below them, he would be okay.

He was, after all, Kait's "water dog." When Kait gave him the nickname, she didn't mean it as in an axolotl. Marissa once purchased an axolotl. She had a freshwater, tropical fish phase and found the axolotl at a pet store. A few months in, it started hanging out at the top of the tank and wouldn't swim with the other fish. Apparently, it lost the use of its gills. Even though everything they had read said an axolotl couldn't survive outside of water, when they placed it in a low bowl in a terrarium, it crawled onto land and stayed there. In the end, Jules cared for the axolotl because it liked live earthworms. Marissa, despite all her experience in the kitchen with various meats, couldn't handle wiggly worms. He then learned she would cry when they boiled living lobsters.

These thoughts made him smile. Suddenly as his thoughts drifted toward the melancholy, he wondered, if he was like that axolotl, with his attachment to the water and his unnatural transformation that made sense but didn't—did that make Minette a salamander?

As far as he understood, each elemental guardian (earth, air, water and fire) called a werewolf to aid in its work controlling the creative force of the universe. There had to be more wolves, because it didn't seem likely that out of four wolves two came from the same family. Or maybe all the wolves shared genetic material. Maybe the extra DNA only existed in one genetic line and the breeding patterns of that line had caused mutations, or maybe the line was dying out, and nature was finding new ways to help them survive.

How the hell should he know?

Jules inhaled deeply and imagined that he could draw the breath all the way into his toes, and for emphasis, he wiggled them. Tensing and relaxing the muscles in his body as close to one-by-one as he could muster slowed his racing heart and trembling nerves.

A compartment opened somewhere in front of him.

"All of these movies are James Bond," Benji muttered. "Except for this... Zazie?"

Jules kept breathing and performing his muscular inventory. With each movement in the cabin distracting him, Jules opened his eyes. Benji had selected a movie. He wrestled it from the case and into the DVD player. Jules closed his eyes, but wondered about Minette. He opened his eyes again, and checked on her, at least visually. She appeared to be asleep. Which, considering he had just given her a substantial dose of tranquilizer and anti-psychotic, meant the "medicine" was working.

It also meant he was running low on Dad's special pills. The James Bond theme song filled the passenger compartment as Jules sighed and closed his eyes again. From the brief glimpse he had, it had to be a newer James Bond. Definitely not Connery.

The plane rattled and whirred. The jet engines made metallic vibrations. The whole machine worked in a cacophonous chorus. Jules exhaled and pried his clenched teeth apart. Until recently, he had worked in commercial kitchens, in restaurants with great reputations. He had climbed his way through the ranks, and served as sous-chef under a demanding head chef without metaphorically breaking a sweat. (In the kitchen, you couldn't avoid breaking a real sweat. Removing perspiration stains from white jackets was its own art form.)

But this... with his siblings on a private jet... His muscles refused to relax no matter how much he willed them otherwise. The movie annoyed him. The growls of the plane echoed within his ears. He fought the urge to growl in return. He repeated the exercise from earlier, tensing and relaxing each muscle as his own meditation.

"Jules!"

The scream came from his brother's mouth. He thrust his eyes open, and from the groggy heaviness in his body, Jules knew he must have fallen asleep.

"Jules!"

He turned toward the call. An unfamiliar intensity overcame him. Jules realized that his own emotions had been overpowered by the panic in his brother. Benji stood in the aisle. The old cliché was true— the color had drained out of him, and he had transformed into an odd shade of olive. Jules wondered if that's what jaundice looked like. Jules parted his lips about to ask if his brother was okay, when clearly he already knew that his brother was not.

But then his senses washed past his brother. Minette laid stiffly in her chair, laid seemed the most accurate word as she certainly no longer sat. Her body twisted and convulsed both spastic and seizing. Jules jolted from his chair, only to be strangled through the abdomen by his seat belt. He unfastened it.

The bones in the upper portion of his sister's skull rolled inward and upward, her skin rippling like heaving ocean waves. Her nose had stretched into the snout of a wolf but still maintained human flesh. Her fingers had curled inward into fists and claws extended from the middle knuckles. Fluid dripped from her eyes like tears but it had a burnt color like diluted blood and pus.

Jules couldn't focus. He didn't understand. In ten years of dealing with the transformation, he had never experienced this. What was happening? How could he help? Could anyone help? Was Minette in danger?

"Tell Captain Luc we need to land the plane," Jules told his brother with unexpected staidness.

"What do I say?" Benji asked frantically.

Suddenly, his mind cleared and he could hear the reassuring, confident voice of Jacqueline in her doctor mode.

"Minette is having a serious seizure and medication isn't helping," Jules said.

Benji staggered toward the cockpit. Jules reached into his pocket for the last of the pills, confirming the presence of the bottle and jiggling it just enough to hear the remaining contents rattle. He scanned the plane for something to grind them. He didn't want her to choke. His thoughts of dread kept repeating, and that didn't help any of them. His hands and ankles shook wildly as he fought to keep himself upright and steady. Whatever his fears right now, Minette needed him.

Jules rushed to the liquor cabinet. He seized the heaviest bottle he could find, a bulbous crystal decanter. He had three pills left in the orange bottle. He gazed to poor Minette, her eyes now open wide and pleading with him. He grabbed a cocktail napkin from the decorative basket atop the cabinet and dumped the remaining pills onto the cabinet top. Using the decanter as a pestle, Jules pressed firmly but gently and rotated the bottle, slowly increasing the pressure and speed of his movement.

He grabbed a nearby glass, held it below the cabinet and dumped the chunks and dust from the custom-compounded pills into the glass. He took a bottle of vodka, carefully drizzling only enough to make a thick paste into the glass. He mixed the concoction with a crystal cocktail stirrer, no gaudy plastic swords here. For good measure, he brought the vodka bottle to his lips and chugged a hearty serving before returning it to its companions. He grabbed a spoon.

He had to tell Dad. He couldn't keep hiding this. Minette's experience with her werewolfism, or as Jacqueline would say 'inherited lycanthropic disorder,' it was different than his. Jules moved toward Minette with his medicated, vodka paste.

Benji returned from the cockpit.

"Captain Luc is trying to find an airport," Benji said. "We're lucky we're not in the middle of the Atlantic."

The two of them met directly over Minette.

"Okay, Min," he told her.

She stared at him, if that's what you called it. She didn't really have a choice. Her eyes were wide but gaping from misshapen holes in her skull. Human eyes normally sat in large round sockets. Minette's sockets had shrunk, pushing toward her chin and elongated nose, creating more room in the forehead area as if her brain had started creeping forward. Her nose had literally stretched and thickened. She now had a snout the length of his finger, and the cute soft tip of her human nose now had a dark, mottled texture. Her nostrils faced forward now instead of below. They flittered constantly. Jules knew she had no choice but to sniff them.

"I can't," Benji muttered as he fell into a chair on the other side of the aisle.

"Min," Jules repeated. "I want you to try as hard as you can to follow my directions. I'm going to put this in your mouth and I just want you to think of every part of your body, one at a time, try and tense those muscles and relax them. Start at your toes."

Jules slowly but rhythmically dished the mixture into her mouth, mere droplets at a time. He didn't want the vodka to overwhelm her and burn her throat. Her features twisted to indicate that it tasted terrible, even her distorted features couldn't hide that. Jules stifled a nervous chortle. Minette's seizures slowed, but her stiffness and disfiguration did not. Jules sat beside her and reached for her misshapen hand.

"Close your eyes and feel the inside of your body," Jules said. "Find the peace within it."

Minette closed her eyes, but as she did, Jules absorbed a vibe from her. Even in her distress, her sassy, little sister energy came into him.

"Yes," Jules said rather curtly. "I know exactly how ridiculous it sounds."

Captain Luc announced that he had successfully diverted the plane to New York and they would start the descent as soon as air traffic control gave them the signal. But what would they do when they landed? Go to a hospital? How would they explain Minette's appearance? Call their father? Book a hotel?

Jules cracked his neck. Something needed to interrupt the silence and his racing thoughts.

CHAPTER TEN

No one on the plane seemed comfortable. Minette remained stiff and unyielding, unable to sit fully in the chair. Benji looked like a panicked dog. And Jules— he maintained a rock-steady exterior, but internally even his organs vibrated.

As soon as the wheels bounced against the runway, Jules' phone rang. He flipped it open, surprised to see the ID on the screen.

"What really happened?" Basilie asked, without even a perfunctory hello.

"How did you—"

"It's a private jet, and I write the checks," she interrupted. "I probably got the memo before the airport."

"Minette," he said. "She was seizing and frozen in some state I don't recognize."

"Oh good," she replied.

A second of awkwardness passed as Jules wondered if his employer had lost her humanity.

"I knew your sister had health issues, but I didn't know if that was covering up something more... serious."

They both went silent. Okay, so she was concerned that something supernatural was going on. She had had the least exposure to the depth of the situation.

"No," Jules said. Though he wasn't sure if that were the correct answer.

Should he tell her more? If everyone else had withheld information, was he really the one to start telling the truth? Guilt suddenly filled him.

"A driver is meeting you at the airport," Basilie said. "I've arranged for Étienne's regular rooms."

"Regular rooms?"

"Chez d'Amille always entertains guests at The Peninsula. We have a suite on retainer."

"Of course," Jules said. That's why when Étienne went to Chicago, he automatically went to that hotel. "And if you talk to Jacqueline..."

Her sister knew more than his boss did. How was that fair? What could he ask Basilie? 'Excuse me, Madame, but can you tell your sister we're having uncontrolled werewolf issues?' Maybe Basilie shouldn't know how little they all understood about their own lives.

"I will alert her," Basilie said.

The line went dead. The plane came to a stop. Benji went to Minette, who cautiously rotated her arm. She whimpered and stared at her distended hand, offered a guttural noise and moved her jaw, but no words came from her mouth. She grunted, and her eyes met with Jules' pleading with him. She didn't have to speak to convey how trapped she felt in her own mutated skeleton.

Jules scooped her upward, allowing her to wrap a freakish arm around his neck and rest it on his shoulder as Benji slipped beneath her other side. She arranged her feet on the floor, and Jules wondered what her limbs looked like under her clothes and her shoes.

"You okay?" he asked her.

Her eyes went wide and her lips, as disfigured as they were, somehow Jules knew they had turned into a pout. Benji grabbed a blanket from a nearby chair and arranged it over her head and shoulders like a hood.

"Min, we'll figure it out," Jules said.

They deplaned down a staircase, with Minette stumbling with every step. Then, they were ushered through what seemed to be a private terminal to a sleek, black limousine glimmeringly clean even in the darkness. A uniformed driver opened the door and helped Captain Luc with their meager luggage. Jules scanned the empty blacktop and surrounding buildings, disturbed by the expansive "smallness."

"This isn't New York City," Jules said quietly to Benji.

"It's Teterboro," their driver said. "Outside Hackensack. New Jersey."

The driver surveyed Minette, dangling between them. Jules' thoughts raced with the need for a cover story, a reason their sister would be twisted and deformed.

"Is... that... one of those abandoned Russian orphans that needs plastic surgery?" the driver asked.

Jules froze. This is when he realized the power of the human mind's urge to rationalize.

"She's scheduled to see a specialist in the morning," he confirmed.

The driver nodded. And in that moment, Jules turned to Benji and almost shrugged but caught himself. If people could so easily explain away something so obviously not right, how could they also be so religious?

"You're headed to the Peninsula. Someone must like her," the driver said.

"It's a Make-A-Wish thing," Benji blurted.

The driver nodded again and waved them impatiently toward the car. Suddenly Jules understood another truth: the more resources you have, the less people ask questions.

During the drive, Minette's face shifted closer to normal. Her features appeared extreme, but at least they appeared human. Her breathing was less strained. Jules reached for her hand. Less hair on the fingers, less rigid in the joints. Whatever had happened to his sister had slowly started to reverse. Jules exhaled.

The Peninsula stood proudly adorned with various flags, a boring slab of gray against a similarly dark Manhattan block. The staff, adorned in white from pill-box hat to gloves, busied themselves inside the building and out, artificial more than posh in Jules' opinion. Perhaps because he spent most of his career dressed in impractical white with weird hats.

The bellhop gathered their luggage: Jules' duffel, Benji's carry-on and back-pack, Minette's backpack and the small travel trunk Étienne's employees had put together. Everything sat sadly on the cart, out of place with the assortment of matching luggage and high-end names. People in suits, women meticulously put together with perfect hair, trending make-up and matching accessories passed through the lobby, itself full of neutral colors and bright light. The setting proved a stage for the wealth on display.

The three of them approached the check-in desk. He and his brother still helped their hobbling sister, who struggled with every step. He shuddered. Jules never liked to attract attention. In their averageness, they stood out. Even the desk staff stared.

"I believe we have a reservation," Jules muttered.

A check-in clerk stepped to the counter. His name tag read 'Edward.'

"Name?"

"We are guests of Madame Basilie d'Amille," Jules said.

"Oh," Edward said. "Mr. Zweigenbaum, welcome."

Edward prepared key cards and placed them on the edge of the counter.

"We have prepared the normal Chez d'Amille accommodations for you. And…"

Edward gestured toward another man.

"Michael will be your personal concierge."

Personal concierge? Jules gazed to the man.

"Anything you need, this…"

Edward held up a business card and slipped it into the folder with the keys.

"… is Michael's number."

Jules reached for the folder, but before his fingers struck the paper, a dark, masculine hand swept across the counter retrieving it. The hand belonged to a navy blue sleeve with a crisp, pink pencil stripe on the cuff of a shirt. Then, the man who owned the hand breezed out from behind the counter, presenting himself to the group with a stoic nod. In a coordinated but unspoken gesture, the bellhop fell in line with the luggage and the pair turned toward the elevator.

"Hello," the man, who turned out to be rather short, said.

"Michael?" Jules said.

"Who else?" Michael replied.

Michael had a bald head, a gold hoop in his earlobe, and a navy blue tie with polka dots. At the moment, Jules couldn't help but look at his shoes. Étienne had trained Jules well. And Michael wore a pebble-grained brogue in blue that Étienne would like, and perhaps comment that the size of his feet did not match his smaller stature. That made Jules look again, as Michael led the siblings toward their room. They all piled into the elevator, and Jules had to admit that despite his small size and well-tailored suit, Michael appeared to be stockier than Jules had first assumed.

Minette's weight eased against Jules' shoulder as she supported herself more. Michael led the group through gleaming hallways with a focused trajectory. Eventually, they reached their destination, which Jules foolishly thought was a room. Michael opened a broad set of double doors and corralled them into another, and a private, hallway.

"The master suite is just there to the left," he proclaimed, waving his hand. "The kitchen is here to the right."

Jules turned his head and sure enough, there was a small but full kitchen to his right. And it had a very high-end refrigerator.

"Behind you," Michael said with another gesture. "Is a third bedroom that we've attached to the suite for your convenience. The other bedroom is beyond the dining room."

"Exactly how big is this suite?" Jules asked.

"Three-thousand square-feet," Michael replied, "without the extra deluxe suite attached."

Jules choked on the perfectly climate-controlled air.

"Where would you like your bags?" Michael asked.

"Uh," Benji croaked. "The master suite would be fine."

"Very good," Michael replied.

Upon eye contact from Michael, the bellhop moved their belongings down a long hallway with several more double doors. He soon disappeared beyond the doors in front of them, veering to the left.

"Let's continue the tour," Michael said.

"I'd like to," Minette growled, "lie down."

"Of course," Michael said.

Micheal directed them in the same path of the bellhop, ushering them into a spacious study that overlooked Fifth Avenue. Paintings, a television, a chair of golden velvet, and a oblong corner love seat that stared at a sleek desk and white leather captain's chair. Michael directed Minette to the next room, where she staggered to a luxurious, fluffy white bed as the bellhop piled their bags on the ottoman. With the luggage and Minette settled, the bellhop departed and Michael continued the tour.

He slipped through another door in the study, which opened into the living room, complete with grand piano. Michael showed them the controls for the television and the thermostat. Benji plopped onto an oversized chair and did not follow them out. Once in the main hall again, Michael pointed out a powder room on the right and the second bedroom on the left, with its own bathroom. Farther toward the entrance of the suite, they reached the dining room (opposite the study) which seated eight for formal dining. With a noticeable bounce in his step, Michael turned into the kitchen. Someone played "Twinkle Twinkle Little Star" haltingly on the piano.

"How do you deal with all this?" Jules blurted.

"Pardon me, sir?" Michael asked.

The bellhop zipped down the hall with the luggage rack. Benji lagged behind, checking behind each open door.

"First off, I'm not a sir," Jules said, as he leaned against the counter by some alien coffee machine. "I'm the d'Amille's chef. So we're peers, in the same game, catering to rich people."

Michael gave him a serious but complicit look.

"This is a lot," Jules said.

Michael made a soft, reassuring toss with his hands. "My advice would be to enjoy it. Your employer booked it for you."

"This is not my vibe," Jules said.

"Do I need to find you something else?" Michael asked.

"Of course not, this is amazing. It's just not what I'm used to."

Benji turned into the kitchen, making the room suddenly feel much smaller.

"Is there anything I can do to make your stay more pleasurable?" Michael asked.

"Yeah," Benji bellowed. "There's a restaurant, with a younger chef. Her name is Marissa Moorehouse. Do you think you can arrange a dinner for my brother?"

Michael gave him whale eye.

"Do you know the name of said restaurant?" he asked.

Benji rubs his chin. Jules wanted to hit him.

"It escapes me."

"I will see what I can do," Michael said.

"That won't be necessary," Jules said.

"I think it is," Benji replied. "Where did you say she worked last?"

Jules exhaled sharply through his nose. He clenched his jaw.

"She loves *haute* vegan cuisine. Last I heard, she had left Paris for a sous-chef position at Good Gravy Carrot," Jules said.

Michael offered an overstated blink. "I can work with that."

"Thank you," Benji said as he encouraged Michael toward the door of the suite.

The door closed with the hotel staff on the other side of it. Benji gave Jules that askance gaze that siblings give each other.

"Dude," he said. "We're in Manhattan. You can't just sit here."

"My sister needs me," he replied.

"I can look after her," Benji said.

Silence.

"You should find Marissa."

"Why?" Jules snapped.

"Because it's been five years, and you still love her."

"Four," Jules replied staidly.

Somehow, Micheal the concierge performed the miracle. He secured a 9:30 p.m., table for one reservation for Jules at a trendy vegan spot, Harmless NYC, where a certain Marissa Moorehouse had attracted the attention of the culinary media in Manhattan. Armed with this information, Jules knew he needed to get cleaned up. He brought his sack to the second bedroom. Benji would take the attached deluxe room on the other end of their suite.

Jules selected a clean pair of black jeans and a simple fitted dress shirt. He hadn't asked Michael if there was a tie requirement, but Michael did say that the hotel's car service would be waiting for him at 9 p.m. He showered, shaved, and arranged his hair into a low ponytail, as he often did. He crossed the hall to the living area, where Benji had an old episode of *Buffy the Vampire Slayer* on television.

"It seemed appropriate," Benji said.

"What episode is it?" Jules asked.

"They have Oz chained in the basement," Benji said. "They just figured out he's the werewolf."

"Benji, don't be an ass."

"I'm not," Benji said. "You'll see as soon as the commercial ends."

Jules scowled. "Just don't let your sister see that. She's upset enough."

Jules snaked through the hall, into the study and into the master bedroom. Minette sat at the head of the bed propped on pillows. She looked like herself, her big brown eyes, her cute nose, and the same oval face that they all shared. Her cheeks had a strong flush to them. Her skin still seemed pale in the hotel lighting. But the fluffy comforter and collection of pillows had a coziness to them. And she smiled.

"Hey," he said softly.

"Hey," her voice sounded raspy. She reached for a bottle of Perrier on the nightstand. "That's Fifth Avenue out the window."

"I know," he told her.

"I didn't," she said. "The last few hours is a massive blur."

"So you have no idea what happened?" he asked.

Her face dropped, and a tear gathered in her eye. When he met her gaze, he felt such heavy pain.

"I was stuck," she said. "Has that ever happened to you? I was stuck in that in-between place of heartbeats and adrenaline. My bones breaking... or something."

His stomach turned, and the ache in his chest chilled him. He knew. He knew exactly the place. He called it 'the final moment of consciousness.' It was the point of the shift where he left his human self behind, but his body still struggled with the transformation. No one else understood the power of the change. There was a part of him that clung to the animal, thrived on instinct, but— thanks to Jacqueline— he had learned to channel it instead of medicate it. Minette had somehow gotten trapped in an in-between world, only slightly animal in physical form but her human self gone.

"How did it happen?" Jules asked.

"I don't know," she said. "One second I was buckling my seatbelt... I remember take-off... but the rest..."

"You're okay now?"

She exhaled and offered a slight shrug of her shoulder, hand tight against the neck of the Perrier bottle.

"But... you feel..."

"Human," she whispered. "I'm shaken, but I'm me."

"Sleep," Jules directed her, placing his hand on the leg-shaped bump under the covers. "Your body needs to rest and recover."

"Jules," she replied. "Am I broken?"

"I don't think so," he said. "I'll keep an eye on you. And Benji's here."

"Why is this happening?" she asked.

"Why are you so dramatic?" he responded, faking some sarcastic energy.

"I don't want to be a werewolf," she said.

"Yeah," he said with a chuckle. "Neither do I."

"Benji said you're going out to dinner with Marissa."

"Not exactly," he grumbled. "Benji asked the hotel concierge to find Marissa and make me a reservation for dinner."

"You look nice," she said.

"Thanks," he said.

"You hoping to win her back?"

"Min," he said, "she left when she found out what I am. That hasn't changed."

"I don't know," she said. "You might not see it, but you've changed. I can't label it exactly. But when we were kids, Dad taught us that the wolf was a monster. Somehow, you proved him wrong."

"Did I?" he said.

"Well, you are the only reason I'm not losing my shit right now."

Jules smiled. "I'll take that."

The trip to the restaurant was a blur of honking horns and blurred lights across New York City streets. The ambiance of the restaurant itself was modest and clean, a tribute to its efforts to leave no carbon footprint and to eliminate food waste. Jules scoffed at the very idea. But before long, he found the dishes that sounded most like Marissa and ordered.

Eight artfully round ravioli sat on the plate coated with a richly brown sauce speckled with candied pecans. A ring of dried kale circled them, a dark green splash beside a pool of earth tones. As the platter steamed, maple aroma hung in the air punctuated by cinnamon. And when he tasted it, Jules realized even the kale had been sugared.

It's like vegetable candy, he thought.

He sliced into the ravioli, revealing a vibrant orange interior. He smeared the morsel on his fork through the sauce and made sure he scooped a candied pecan onto his first bite. The blend of maple syrup and something buttery made a powerful complement for the sweet potato ravioli. The filling had just enough cinnamon to foster a zing across the taste buds, to calm the sweet blend of vegetables and sugars.

And he remembered, once upon a time, her trying to perfect raviolis like these in their kitchen. At that time, she was experimenting with a gluten-free variation by creating a custard with the sweet potato filling, that she put in a ramekin, with the candied pecans as a topping and the sauce drizzled on top.

At the time, he told her she couldn't cook for everyone.

"Maybe I can," she had told him.

When Marissa walked out of the kitchen, even with a flushed face and the weight of a full day bringing fatigue into her eyes, hair pulled back under a sweat-stained bandana, her chef's jacket partially deflated and wrinkled, but still mostly crisp... four years older and she still stirred warmth in him. He knew that he denied his heartache when she left, but seeing her again really emphasized it.

"So it really is you," she said. "When the Peninsula called and said they had a guest looking for me, word got to me."

"It was an unexpected visit," he said. "I'm supposed to be in Chicago."

"There's an Italian spot across the street," she said. "You want to get some spiked coffees? It's more private..."

"After that meal? I didn't think you would ever make ravioli that amazing. I didn't think anyone could. But you did," he replied. "Coffee sounds great."

She blushed. He hoped it was in response to his compliments. She led him across the street where they selected a small table with upholstered chairs in a lounge space beside the bar outside the dining room. The main walkway extended behind them, a four-foot wall separating them from those coming it to eat. The mini-wall displayed a hodgepodge of Catholic imagery, from prints of Middle Ages religious portraits with dark gold halos to photos of historic churches and chapels.

"So," she said, fidgeting with the delicate spoon. "How did you become a werewolf? Why did I never know? Did something happen? Because we spent plenty of full moons together."

He laughed, perhaps more boisterously than he should have. Frank Sinatra sang in the background. Several tables still had diners. The bar was full. But even in the dim light and across the distance, Jules could still make out the white marble top with its dark veins between the drinkers snacking on a bizarre mix of fried sage leaves, prosciutto and salami, olives and scaldatelli, ring-shaped, fennel-flavored crackers. In front of them, they had a small basket of mini-biscotti aromatically filling the air with notes of almond and amaretto.

"As strange as this sounds," Jules said. "I always had the condition. It surfaced when we moved to California. My dad blames the stress of the move."

Marissa froze, confusion wrinkled her face.

"Like a disease?" she said.

"It's a recessive inherited disorder, with wolf DNA intertwined with the male chromosome. Sexual maturity and hormones typically activate it. Not much is known about it, but it's what brought my parents together."

"So is your dad..."

"No," he quickly said. "Just a carrier."

"Benji?"

Jules shook his head. "But, somehow, Min got it, but that's supposed to be impossible."

They chit-chatted for a while, which was hard because Jules kept obsessing over how good she looked and how jovial she seemed, and Jules finally had to ask.

"There's no one else?"

"I tried," she said, sipping her Irish-creme-laced cappuccino.

"I've learned a lot about myself since you left," he said. "Maybe when I take care of this Chicago trip, you would let me spoil you a bit."

She nodded slowly. "No promises about the future."

"Lord, don't I know."

CHAPTER ELEVEN

By the time Jules rose the next morning, Benji had somehow acquired a video game system and sat rapt on the sofa. The aroma of coffee filled the halls and music— a little more lively and air-headed than he was used to— accompanied it. It was nearly 10 a.m. Jules hadn't slept this late in ages. He found Minette in the kitchen of the suite.

Minette, now in one of the dresses from her custom trousseau, a soft pink-and-white gingham affair with a high waist and a tight skirt that ended just above the knee, handed him a mug as he moved into the kitchen. The gingham said country while the skirt said secretary.

"What are you doing in the kitchen?" Jules asked.

She pointed to a cumbersome machine that resembled a shrunken garbage can with dark plastic pieces attached to a water tank of some kind. She held up some small tubs, like giant creamer packets with foil lids.

"It's an individual coffee machine," she said.

She pointed to the words on the front, Keurig, and pronounced it with a ridiculous German accent.

"It's not German," he said as he smelled the contents of the mug.

He tasted it. It was coffee. Not fresh ground, not good coffee, but coffee.

"How are you feeling?" he asked.

"Good," she answered. "Shaky, but I think that's emotional."

"Do you want breakfast?"

"I ate some stuff out of this," she said.

She pointed to a wicker basket that housed a banana and some shortbread cookies.

"Okay," she continued. "I ate most of the basket."

"I can cook something, or we could order room service, or we could find a nice, New York diner."

"I don't think we have the time to be tourists," she reminded him.

He nodded.

"So should I cook?" he asked.

"That depends," she replied. "Are you still a vegetarian?"

He exhaled. "Look, my theory is that behaving like a carnivore encouraged the wolf. You might consider it."

"Or perhaps some juicy meat would keep the wolf satisfied."

"Is that what happened on the plane? Not enough steak?"

She glared at him. "I don't know what happened on the plane."

He turned to the fridge and opened the door. To his surprise, there was a gallon of whole milk, a fancy cheese platter, a dozen eggs and some miscellaneous fruits and vegetables. He found a block of butter, good butter, too, and a dark chocolate bar. He closed the door.

"I'll make omelets," he replied, as he set down his mug and started rooting around the kitchen for pans and utensils.

"How long will we be here?" she asked.

With a silicone turner dangling from his hand, Jules shrugged.

"I didn't exactly plan this," he said.

She nodded.

"So if there is anything else you can tell me..." he added.

She lifted a mug. "I'm scared."

Jules piled ingredients on the counter beside the fridge. He kept his attention on the eggs and the cheese.

"We should talk to Dad," he said.

"No," she boomed.

"How else are we going to get answers?" he asked.

"There has to be other people," she replied. "What about those guardian folks? What about your doctor friend?"

Jules brought down a bowl from the cupboard. Adeptly, and almost silently, he cracked eggs into the bowl and tossed empty shells into the sink. He lost count, the rhythm soothing him. He couldn't find a whisk, so he whipped them as best he could with a spoon.

"She sent a text," he said. "She's reviewing her notes and will call around lunchtime, as soon as she gets done with her shift at the hospital."

He sliced a generous pat of butter and dropped it into the frying pan. The two of them ate cheese omelets silently with Benji. Suddenly, Benji moved his chair to the head of the long dining table. He performed some sort of skit amid the upholstered chairs and view of the Manhattan streetscape. It might have been a scene from *Arthur*.

Jules' phone vibrated. It pulled it from his pocket, read Jacqueline's name as it scrolled across the display, excused himself from the table and went into the study.

"Hello?" he answered, falling into his natural language of French. "Jacqueline? Do you have news?"

"Perhaps," she said. "Do you remember when we flew together?"

"It was two months ago. Of course, I remember."

"You're not usually this sassy," she replied.

"I'm worried."

"When we can't help family members, it's the worst feeling," Jacqueline said.

She let him stew in silence. Or, at least, that's how it felt.

"I looked at my notes..."

She constantly scribbled and sketched on the blank pages of that notebook. The texture of the paper inside reminded him of a modernized parchment and she used the fanciest pens.

"... and I did some reflecting and even brainstorming. I examined the notes from our sessions, and how your medication impacted you. And I thought about my personal experiences with you..."

He wondered if that meant she had been thinking about the rough sex they had in the back of a military truck in the desert.

"... and the recent tests."

"Okay."

What else could he say?

"You told me that you were afraid of flying," she said.

He shuddered. "I hate flying."

"What if I told you you don't?" she said.

Even though it was a phone call, Jules curled his lip and muffled a snarl.

"I think I know my own phobias."

"Jules?" Minette called from the other room. "Who is it?"

He covered the phone.

"Doc Saint," he returned.

"You don't have aviophobia," she said. "Here's my theory. It's a symptom of lycanthropy."

She never called him a werewolf.

"It's not triggered by fear," she explained. "You're fine getting on the plane and even take-off. You're nervous because of anticipation of what happens during the flight."

"That still sounds like fear of flying," he said.

"Hear me out. When the plane gains altitude, the oxygen levels and air pressure change. The cabin is pressurized, it's why we don't suffocate when we fly. It's different from the air on the ground."

"Jacq, can we get to the point?"

"Your wolf DNA activates mid-flight because your body detects the change in air pressure and oxygen levels and sees it as a threat to your survival. Your body sees the mechanical air flow as an asphyxiation risk."

"Jacq, can you dumb this down? Why did my sister get stuck mid-transformation?"

"I don't know," she admitted, "but I am fairly confident that flying will trigger a shift into wolf form for both of you."

"That's all you've got?"

"My best advice is not to fly."

"Then how do I get to Chicago?"

"Drive?" she replied.

He sighed.

"I'm a great gynecologist," Jacqueline said. "And I'm a damn good combat surgeon. I'm sorry my experience with horny soldiers, body trauma and STIs doesn't always translate easily into lycanthropic disorders."

He smiled. "Because horny soldiers and werewolves are so similar."

"And don't forget vaginas."

He appreciated her attempt to lighten the mood. And as he thought about it, her newest clue made sense. And perhaps it gave them more insight than he realized. At least she treated them like people and not freaks.

"I try not to," he said.

"Good," she said. "You're a great guy, Jules. You need to see more vaginas."

"Thank you, Doctor," he replied. "But since I started working for your family, I'm starting to think vaginas are dangerous."

"They are," she replied. "Talk to you soon."

The conversation ended and Jules returned to the dining room. His siblings looked at him, frozen like schoolchildren waiting for news. He put the phone in his pocket.

"Well, guys," he said. "I think I need to ask our friend Michael to rent us a car. According to Jacqueline, the wolves think flying will kill them."

"Is that what happened to me?" Minette asked.

"Yes and no," he replied. "You got stuck. We still don't know why. So we're not going to put you on a plane."

CHAPTER TWELVE

Michael had promised he would call Étienne's regular car service and have something for them to drive to Chicago later that day. Jules was torn— logic said to leave in the morning when they had a good night's sleep, but instinct led to urgency telling him to leave as soon as possible.

Benji and Minette had decided to explore Manhattan for a couple hours, and they deserved that.

Jules stayed behind. Someone should wait for the car and make preparations for their road trip.

For now, Jules stared out the window, watching the traffic and passersby on Fifth Avenue. He went over recent events again. Étienne had gone to Chicago. Jules wanted to know why. And his gut said that Kait was with him. The photos that had appeared in recent tabloids suggested that Adelaide, or someone that looks like her, had joined them.

Jules couldn't sense Kait yet, as he did when she was physically close, but if he listened hard enough, his body could feel the pull. The wolf in him had a connection with her and would always point to her— like a compass or an alert dog.

Jules paced the long edge of the room, never breaking his stare from the window. No one had addressed the other major issue with this situation. No one had discussed the obvious: Had Adelaide come back from the dead? If so, how? Why?

The phone in his pocket vibrated wildly. He retrieved it, gazed at the screen, smiled, and answered it.

"Coucou, Marissa," he greeted her.

She made a soft little noise that was almost a giggle.

"I haven't spoken real French in a long time," she said.

"Only kitchen French?"

She chuckled.

"I just wanted to thank you," she said. "I'm glad we had a chance to talk while you were in town."

"It felt good," Jules said. "I never thought the day would come when I could be honest with anyone."

"So are you leaving this morning?" she asked.

"We're waiting on a rental car," Jules replied. "Gives Benji and Min a chance to play in the city. I don't think Benji has been to New York."

"It's Monday, if you wanted to play in the city."

Jules pulled the phone away from his ear. Did she just say... Did he hear a seductive tone in her typically no-nonsense voice?

"I already made breakfast," he said. "And I don't think we'll be here long enough for a show."

"Your hotel has a beautiful rooftop terrace and indoor pool," she told him, "and I believe a full service spa."

"Does it?" he replied.

Was this informational? Or was she fishing for an invitation?

"It does," she said.

He nodded. "Would you like me to reach out to Michael and send a car for you?"

"Why, Mr. Zweigenbaum, a car?"

Part of him worried that Basilie would examine the bill and question the expenses, but how much could a town car cost, or was it included? This room— no, this apartment— had to cost $20,000 a night. He went into the study and rang for Michael. He put the phone on speaker and kept Marissa on the line on his cell phone.

"This is Michael."

"Good morning, Michael."

"Good morning, Mr. Zweigenbaum."

"Really, Michael? So formal?"

"Good morning, Jules. I hope the room has been satisfactory."

"It has. Would you be able to send a car for a friend of mine?" Jules asked.

"Certainly, sir. All I need is the address."

Details provided, Jules disconnected the call.

"Well, then," Marissa said. "Someone has moved up in the world."

Now, Jules chuckled. "Come on over. We can pretend we're rich people for a while."

When that call ended, Jules realized he needed to get ready. He didn't know exactly what Marissa intended— to be a good host and show off her new hometown? To reconnect because they were engaged once? To test if their chemistry had survived?

He hadn't packed for the occasions now arising. He had worn his dress shirt last night so now opted for a simple white t-shirt. When the knock on the door came, he was barefoot, in his black jeans and his tee. He opened the door to find that one of the hotel's crisp, white toy soldier employees had escorted Marissa to him. The employee offered a bow gesture and retreated. Jules smiled and ushered Marissa into the suite.

She stepped across the threshold. "This is not a room."

"It is not," he said. "It's not even an apartment. It's something far more."

Marissa held a black clutch purse and wore black-sequined heels with an above-the-knee, plunging neckline wrap dress in forest green satin. She had pulled her dark, wavy hair into a messy updo, but the only make-up she had on was mascara and red lipstick.

"You look amazing," he said.

"I don't get the chance to hob-knob often," she replied.

When she smiled, he loved the plumpness of her cheeks.

"Well, then... let's not waste the opportunity."

He closed the door. His heart thumped. The urge to wrap his arms around her overwhelmed him with such intensity he had to anchor himself against the floor. "Amazing" did not properly describe her.

"Marissa, may I kiss you?"

"Yes," she said.

He stepped into her, ran one hand over the curve of her cheek, and slipped the other arm around her waist, which was actually closer to the side of her rib cage/breasts because of their height difference, and brought her torso toward him. Their bodies pressed together. He leaned down and brought his lips to hers. Within seconds, their mouths had fallen into a familiar routine of affection and lust.

His body charged. Her familiar scent and taste blinded him. He could feel her body (and his own) warm and smell the musky sweetness of arousal rising in both of them. They were in the eye of a hurricane. Jules considered what his siblings had said.

He did still love her.

She tossed the purse. It may have landed on the kitchen floor as the clunk was not dampened by the carpet. She melted further into him, her muscles dissolving into him with absolute trust. It tortured him to break the hold.

"Marissa," he said. "I never stopped loving you."

Their temples met.

"I thought a lot last night," Marissa said. "And I thought we both deserved another chance."

He kissed her eyebrows.

"You said you wanted to spoil me," she said. "All I've seen is this hallway and I can tell it's excessive in here."

He chuckled. He pulled farther away and threw up his hands in a stop gesture, palms to her.

"This is all my boss," he said. "My version of spoiling you is much more low-key."

She laughed and pushed playfully on his chest.

"I know who you work for," she said. "The whole world knows you work for Étienne d'Amille. Rumors of your dinner parties precede you."

He stepped into her again and renewed his grasp, this time with both hands around her. She sunk into his hold. They kissed, slow and lingering, but his tingling skin and burning nose alerted him that they were both faking their nonchalance.

"Jules," Marissa said softly. "I don't think I've ever... noticed... so much..."

She pushed her thigh into his groin softly, lifting her leg slowly to brush her hip against his erection.

"The medication suppressed a lot of my true feelings," he said.

"Your feelings?" she replied.

He paused, staring into her eyes for a moment before answering.

"Yes, Marissa. My feelings are so much more intense now. I realize how important you are," Jules said. "You're beautiful and so sexy and I have so many memories of us in bed. But this... now... is not just biology or chemistry. It's how I feel."

"I don't know what to say," she whispered.

"Then kiss me again," he replied.

She arched and placed her lips against his, dipping her tongue into his mouth. He inhaled through his nose in a desperate attempt to center himself, because he had to fight the wolf inside him. The wolf wanted to throw her against the wall and impale her mercilessly. His sexual desire for her overwhelmed his rational, appropriately socialized human self.

He swept her from her feet and into his arms. His every thought blurred from the need for her— that step beyond just wanting to claim her and consume her, beyond that place where he released the sense of mourning he had swallowed for four years knowing that he had lost her. His brain reminded him that this might not last, but the animal in him planned to mark her as his territory, both physically and emotionally.

Which he supposed was better than fucking her into oblivion and using her like a sex doll.

She squealed, wrapped her hands around his neck and kissed him as they moved through the what-seemed-longer-than-usual hall to the second bedroom. He placed her on the bed and threw the tousled bedclothes to the floor. He closed his eyes, drawing every scent of her into his depths. He whipped the t-shirt and his pants aside. She smiled and kicked off her shoes.

He grabbed her thighs as she leaned back amid the fluffy pillows and remaining sheet. There was room for him between her knees and he took the space, sliding his hands upward under her sleek skirt, the dance of the satin tickling his hands as his palms treasured her soft flesh. He reached to her hips, then down to her ass, seizing her and pushing her across the mattress.

When they stopped, she pulled the string that held the wrap-dress together and Jules brushed the skirt aside and brought his mouth, and his tongue, against the center of her panties. She moaned, and pressed her fingers into his hair.

And then there was the long-lost but instantly recognizable, salty-milky mix he had almost forgotten. His heart sank.

He propped himself on his elbow at her side.

"You're fertile," he said.

She blinked hard and her eyebrows wrinkled.

"Excuse me?" she said.

"I have to find a condom. You're fertile."

The expression on her face did not change.

"They're in my purse," she said.

Jules dashed down the hall and retrieved the clutch from the kitchen floor. When he returned to the bedroom. Marissa sat cross-legged, dress open and hanging like a robe, revealing a beautiful set of matching black lace bra and panties he had never seen before. He handed her the purse. She opened it. She handed him three condoms in their tiny packages.

"You're optimistic," he said.

She raised her eyebrows.

"Jules," she said. The way she said his name sounded sharp, almost stern.

"What's wrong?" he asked.

"I'm 'fertile'? What is that?"

"You are."

She touched the fingertips of both her hands to her forehead.

"As in... ovulating?" she asked.

"That's when the egg is released, right?" he said. "Because that's what I smell."

"That's what you... smell," she repeated.

He nodded. He placed two of the condoms on the nightstand and held the other. With his other hand, he rubbed his chin.

"I never told you that," he said. "When I'm around certain women often, I can smell the changes in their cycle."

Her eyes widened. "Really?"

He nodded.

"How?" she asked.

He shrugged. "All I know is you smell delicious right now and I haven't tasted a woman in years."

"You haven't slept with anyone since we broke up?"

"Well, I didn't say that," he replied. "I had sex last week. But that was the first time."

"Well, then in comparison," she said. "I was a slut trying to replace you."

They laughed together and wrapped into each other for kisses.

"So you can smell that I might get pregnant," she said.

He nodded.

"That is actually useful," she replied. "And beautiful."

"Beautiful?" he repeated.

She placed her hand on her tummy, cradling the flesh there.

"Well, if we wanted to have a baby, we would know as we... did it... that we really are creating a life."

"Someday," he replied. "Yes."

Jules brushed the hair from her forehead, kissed her again, and traced the pattern of her lace bra. He kissed down her neck, to her shoulder, to her torso, and down her belly. She slid her hand into his hair. Her skin carried the sheen and scent of light sweat and building arousal. He followed it to its core. He removed her panties, gently, and placed his tongue against her.

Instinct drew him into her, the pull of the familiar and the newness of being with her unmedicated proved intoxicating. He trembled, his hands against her thighs, his nose firing madly with the notes of their impending sexual encounter. The intimate taste of her locked his attention on her, and only her, as if the world only existed for her and because of her.

Her writhing and moaning heightened not only his need for her, but heightened the sensation that his worship would claim her and prepare her in a primitive act of not merely pleasure but function. His cock twitched and oozed, as she panted and whimpered. His mouth brought her to an orgasm so hard that she continued to shudder as he stroked her thighs.

He gazed upon her. His erection stood painfully tall as she glistened and glowed before him. Her hair had fallen from its updo. Her juices coated the inside of her legs to her knees and left trails on the sheets. She uncurled her fingers from tight fists.

And then, she laughed.

Jules stood beside the bed. Her ankles hung just slightly past the mattress. He slid her toward him. Jules plunged his eager cock into her, feet strongly on the floor, and together they released a noise that Jules could only label as a howl. He scooped her torso from the bed, bringing him deeper into her and allowing him to fill his mouth with her breast.

Her body collapsed into his arms.

"This is... " she whispered as she fought for the breath to speak, "not what it used to be."

His lips broke from her flesh.

He froze. "Am I hurting you?"

She chuckled. "Oh, God, no."

His shoulders relaxed when he hadn't noticed them tense.

"It's just... better," she said.

He shifted his weight, and he noticed a ripple inside her. Marissa closed her eyes.

"Please," she whimpered. "Keep going."

He moved, testing, wanting to believe her, desperate to release his seed into her. Her body clenched against him as her spine arched. She offered him a musical sigh and Jules knew, as he glided into her and she met him eagerly if not greedily, that he wanted, more than anything, to spend his life with her. He had wondered what seeing her again would do to him, after those years apart. As their bodies thrust against each other, he realized that the decade he had spent suppressing the wolf had not only dulled his emotions but also denied him the certainty that came from his gut when he knew when something was right just as much as he recognized that something was wrong. Instinct. Sharp as knives.

Marissa's moans, breaths and heart rate kept building. Her body shook. She closed her eyes and her body seemed to surrender. Jules closed his eyes and focused on the frequent popping sensations as she gripped him. Her lower body tightened around him, and her whole body erupted in waves. Heat flashed within him. The world turned a deep orange. He fell into her, gorging himself on her breast, toying with her nipple with his teeth, threatening to bite her. She surged toward him, grabbing at his hair, which danced around them wildly. Her vocalizations sounded animalistic, and needy, and desperate.

The pressure of their sexual activity swirled within his every muscle until he erupted with a force he had never known before, his teeth tight against her breast, both his arms wrapped around her, one at the back of her torso and the other around her waist.

Her weight leaned into him, her legs now wrapped around his waist so tight he thought he might bruise, her heels dug into his ass cheeks. Her thighs quivered. Her fingers twisted around locks of his hair. Then, her head dropped like her neck had failed her. Finally, she released a scream that he thought would shatter the windows— but instead her pussy rippled and tightened around him, again, as juices flooded his groin.

Their orgasm hit them with so much force, Jules fell onto the bed.

CHAPTER THIRTEEN

Marissa had collected her clothes and planned to leave the hotel before his siblings returned, but Jules ordered room service. Then, Michael called to say that the rental car would be there in about an hour. Marissa agreed to stay for post-coital, black bean-based burgers smothered in mushroom gravy and Jules promised he would drive her wherever she needed to go and save her the cab fare.

Benji and Minette returned with the requisite amount of "I [heart] NYC" and Big Apple-themed merchandise, and they lamented that they would not have time to catch a Broadway show. Upon seeing Minette, now showered and back in her shimmering green dress, Benji offered a knowing, older brother smirk without even seeing the chaos they had made in the bedroom. If Minette had any thoughts, she hid them well.

Marissa made casual conversation while everyone gathered their belongings in preparation for check-out. Michael confirmed the car had arrived. Benji, Minette, Jules and Marissa strolled into the lobby and Michael— today in a smart, charcoal gray suit with a delicate silvery stripe on his shirt and a floral tie— handed Jules a leather keychain.

"As requested. I called Mr. d'Amille's regular car service," Michael said.

That explained the logo of a "Gotham Dream Cars" on the keychain.

One of the Peninsula's white-gloved footmen ushered them outside. Jules immediately exhaled when he realized what car was "his": long and sleek with a slightly bulbous front end, like some old European racing car, but a modern slightly-cobalt, slightly-navy paint job, tan leather interior you could see from the street, and a cabin that resembled the bastard child of a cockpit and a family sedan.

"Holy shit," Marissa gasped.

Benji walked closer and peered in the window.

"It technically has a backseat, but it's not designed to accommodate legs," he announced.

"What is that?" Minette asked.

"It's an Aston Martin Vanquish," the albino nutcracker explained.

Jules turned to the Peninsula employee.

"We're headed on a road trip," he said. "The three of us."

Jules motioned to his siblings.

"I'm going to drive the lady home," he said. "Do you think you could ask Micheal for something more practical?"

"Of course," the nutcracker replied and headed into the lobby.

"Go... hang out," Jules told Minette and Benji. "I'll be right back."

As if a drive a few miles through Manhattan would only take a minute.

Jules opened the passenger door and held it for Marissa. Marissa eagerly hopped inside. The car growled when Jules got in. He hit the reverse button on the dash after a moment of confusion, switched it back to drive, and pulled it out into the Manhattan traffic.

The drop-off went well, and Marissa kissed him rather luxuriously at her departure. The ride back to the Peninsula allowed him to have fun driving the fanciest car he'd ever seen, even if he could only creep a few car lengths at a time.

His brother and siblings lounged in the Peninsula lobby, their laps covered with plastic sacks of convenience store groceries like the middle-class tourists they were. Jules spotted Michael near the check-in desk. He gave Michael the previous set of keys, but if Jules saw correctly, Michael had a bit of a smirk.

"Oh no," Jules muttered.

"I did my best," Michael said. "But Monsieur d'Amille does not exactly have an account at Hertz or Enterprise."

"Does anyone here?" Jules remarked.

"Do you need to freshen up or shall I alert the staff to bring the car?"

"Do you want us lingering in the lobby?"

Michael stifled a laugh but his eyes betrayed him. Jules gathered his siblings, ignoring the questions and taunts about Marissa's visit. Once again, the toy soldiers-in-white rolled their meager luggage to the curb where they loaded it into a ridiculously long, boxy Rolls Royce in subdued silver, because when the car was a land yacht who needed a flashy paint job?

Unlike the Aston Martin, the Rolls could contain their bags and their legs and even had fold-down trays in the back seat for snack time. Minette, as the youngest, was relegated to the first shift in the rear and she discovered the umbrella built into the suicide door. Within seconds, she called out that she had also discovered a refrigerator, which Benji then passed her their soft drinks to stock it.

"That's a champagne cooler," Jules muttered.

His siblings stared at him. He blushed, suddenly embarrassed that he knew such a fact. The staff at the Peninsula wished him well and Jules hopped into the driver's seat, not sure if what he felt at the moment was relief to have escaped the hotel or apprehension at driving a Rolls Royce across several states— which would no doubt lead to more Arthur jokes from Benji.

He hoped to make it to the Pennsylvania-Ohio border before they stopped for the night. Minette noticed that Mapquest route would take them pretty close to her dorm. She convinced them to detour to Lafayette College. This would allow her to drop off extraneous clothing from the Chez d'Amille staff and stow away her New York treasures, and most importantly give her a chance to collect some clean undergarments.

Two hours later, she dragged Jules and Benji toward a staid, brick building with a clock tower tucked behind a variety of academic buildings. A small parking lot faced the building, and Jules wished she would have let him bring the Rolls Royce right to the door. Judging from the Mercedes and BMWs in the parking garage, this might be the one place where the Rolls would turn less heads.

Across the quad, Minette said, you could walk to the end of the hill and see downtown Easton below them. Soon, the trees would blossom and obscure the view, but for now, the college and the city shared a connection. Jules refused to take a campus tour with her.

"We're on a search and rescue mission," he said.

"And Benji and I really don't need to be a part of it," she snapped.

Minette had no keys or swipe cards since she had teleported across the globe, but luckily a familiar face let her (and them) into the initial strange lobby of the building. She had to explain that she forget her checkpoint in her room, so she managed to get the next door swiped as well. Minette charged through the hall, chattering with renewed energy about her surroundings. She reached for the doorknob to her room, unlocked as she suspected it would be, anxious to greet her roommate.

She froze as soon as she stepped across the threshold. Her fear washed across Jules' senses like an earthquake. Benji stumbled forward, oblivious.

"Oh," he hollered. "And everyone says guys are gross!"

Benji immediately retreated to the hall. Piles of clothes covered the surfaces of the room. They hadn't been created intentionally, but appeared haphazardly tossed and landing into piles because they had nowhere else to go. Books laid askew. But the oddness Jules noticed immediately— both laptops sat quietly on their desks. Why would the laptops still be here if the room had been ransacked? Had the girls been robbed? Or was someone trying to scare them?

"Min," Jules said. "What's going on?"

She turned.

"I have no idea," she said.

"Is anything missing?" he asked.

Minette stepped into the chaos and grabbed keys and a clutch wallet from the desk closest to them. She scanned the contents.

"That's intact," she said. "Down to the two dollars cash I had."

She brushed the clothes from her bed, revealing that the intruders had completely stripped her bed. Jules surveyed the other side of the room. The mess did not extend to that side. He didn't want to suggest it to Minette, but it looked like someone came in, rummaged around enough to determine which things belonged to whom and then focused on his sister. Her roommate's closet still had clothes in it. Minette's items had been tossed to the floor, hangers and all.

Jules exhaled a troubled nasal breath. He certainly was not a detective, but his gut told him that his sister had been the target.

Minette swirled around the small room, her face wrinkled in confusion and her gestures pointed.

"Jules," she said as she paused. "The only thing missing is my dirty laundry."

"Why would someone want your dirty laundry?" Benji said in disbelief. "It's got to be in there somewhere. Maybe you just pissed off your roommate."

Jules grimaced, and now his exhale transformed into a full-blown sigh. Minette's hands offered a slight tremble.

"Jules," Minette said again, in that childhood, baby sister tone that meant she wanted his older brother advice and comfort. "Why would someone steal my dirty laundry?"

"I hope I'm wrong," he replied, "but someone is training dogs to hunt your scent."

"Or it's a pervert wanting to jack off to your dirty underwear," Benji added.

Minette rolled her eyes.

"Great," she said. "Both fantastic options."

"Whatever it is," Jules said, "we should probably keep moving."

"But my roommate," she said.

She counted on her fingers and pointed to a wall calendar.

"Spring break ends tomorrow. She'll be back tonight," Minette said.

Jules sighed again.

"Then let's clean up and leave a note," he said. "Or maybe you should stay here and go to class."

"Someone stole my dirty laundry," she reminded him, "and I am a mutant werewolf. Can we please sort that out before I continue studying water run-off calculations?"

Minette collected some textbooks, pens and her laptop into a backpack. Jules turned, tilted an ear upward and inhaled. The scent of spring penetrated the smells of the college dormitory, among the notes of poignant dirty laundry and powdered chicken broth.

His thoughts mimicked those he had heard Étienne express as he analyzed perfume. Spring had earthy tones— the soil started to smell richer, the reviving grass and shrubbery released "green" into the air. It was probably the gases released by the chlorophyll or something.

Winter had a dampened smell. Even when snow didn't physically cover the ground, the cold temperatures kept everything frozen which prevented the movement that stirred up scents. And right now, Jules could smell the thaw.

"Fine," he said, returning to the present. "Let's get to work."

In the two years Minette had lived on the College campus, he had only visited twice. His life in Paris had made their parents' California home the primary place of reunion. The last time he passed through this town, he was in wolf form, tracking Étienne to the church where he and his musketeers planned on rescuing Adelaide's spirit from the fire mage, Galen.

Benji and Minette tossed items from one end of the room to the other as they tried to arrange them as if nothing had happened. Jules reorganized the closet. His cell phone buzzed. He retrieved it and saw Jacqueline's number flash on the screen. He flipped the phone open and answered in French.

"I just got some reports on your sister," she said, all business and no pleasantries.

"Do they have any answers?" he asked.

"Maybe?" she replied. "But first, can you pass her the phone?"

Jules obeyed. "Min, it's Jacqueline. She wants to talk to you."

Minette took the phone. As Jacqueline talked, Minette's eyes tightened. Her face flushed.

"Yes," she said. "I'm irregular. My mother told me it was because I was too thin."

Benji gazed to Jules as if Jules knew what was happening. Jules shrugged.

"Wow" was all Minette said next.

She lowered herself to the clothing-strewn bed.

"I don't know," she said to Jacqueline.

Minette looked down to one of her breasts, then the other. Or at least, that's what Jules thought. But that would be weird.

"I never thought anything of it," she said.

Her face turned very red. Minette listened a few more minutes.

"Well," Minette said, "that explains that. Thank you."

Minette snapped the phone closed. She handed it to Jules.

"What the hell was that?" Benji exclaimed.

Jules placed the phone in his pocket and massaged his forehead.

"Well," Minette said, slowly standing from the bed. "We're closer to having some answers."

Jules met her eyes. He wanted to be calm. He wanted to protect her.

"So what are they?" Benji yelled.

"The results of all those hormone tests came in," Minette said. "Apparently, I have ridiculously high levels of testosterone."

"So what does that mean?" Jules asked.

Jules didn't like the vibes he was reading from her body. Minette returned his intense gaze.

"It's why I have no real boobs and weird periods," she said. "But is it a real answer?"

"What did Jacqueline say?" Jules asked.

"That we need to wait for the genetic analysis we sent to Dad, but her guess is that the increased testosterone has activated the wolf DNA. She's going to see if she can look at the other test results and make some guesses why I have so much testosterone."

"Do you think Dad ever ran genetic tests on all of us?" Jules asked.

According to Minette, the room looked normal again. Maybe they should have called campus police, or the city police. Nothing made sense. Jules still didn't know why— or perhaps the correct question was how— his sister became a werewolf. He still didn't know if he should bring her, or Benji, to Chicago. But now, seeing that an intruder had broken into her room, he didn't want to leave her behind.

"We have a lot to think about," Jules said. "Let's head out to the car. Maybe stop at McDonald's."

"In a Rolls-Royce?" Minette replied. "Oh, we better go through the drive-thru."

"I could use a burger and fries," Benji said.

"Oh, I'm getting a 20-piece with hot mustard," Minette said.

They headed into the hall and pulled the door closed. Minette locked it. Jules wondered if whoever had entered the room before them would do any harm to her roommate.

"Are you going to share?" Benji asked.

"No," Minette said. "And I'm getting a couple apple pies."

Jules shook his head. "Hey, Min."

"Yeah, Jules?"

"Maybe you should text your roommate and your resident advisor and tell them you think someone was in your room."

"What would that do?"

Jules inhaled. "I'm not sure, but I feel like someone should be on alert, just in case."

"I'm not mentioning the missing underwear," she said.

Minette pulled her phone from her backpack. Her thumbs struck the numbers as she walked toward the parking deck. Benji and Jules walked side by side.

"What are you getting?" Benji asked him.

"At McDonald's? I haven't eaten McDonald's since high school," he replied. "A fish sandwich. Or three, I'm kind of hungry."

CHAPTER FOURTEEN

"The ridiculousness of taking a Rolls-Royce through the McDonald's drive-thru in a questionable neighborhood sure took the edge off. Minette and Benji both climbed into the backseat so they could eat off the fold-down trays. They ordered a heap of chicken nuggets and French fries, not to mention sandwiches, pies and soft drinks, on the Chez d'Amille corporate credit card.

On the passenger seat beside him, Jules sat the MapQuest directions and the atlas Michael had provided. Jules carefully opened the book to the two-page map of Pennsylvania, examining the roadways that criss-crossed the state.

He opened his two Filet-O-Fish sandwiches and stacked two of the patties on one bun, tossing the spare bun into the trash bag. A serenity came over him. Or it might have been a sign that the McDonald's would drop them all into fast food lethargy and they could forget making progress on this journey.

"Hey, Jules," Benji asked, crudely waving his head to camouflage the shreds of McNuggets in his mouth. "I'm the oldest. I can handle a map. Really."

"What's the plan?" Minette asked.

"We'll do shifts driving. The Ohio border is about six hours. If we aim for four-hour shifts, that should get us to Chicago mid-morning," Jules said.

"Unless we stop," Benji said.

"Well, it's a Rolls Royce, we're going to need gas," Jules said.

"Can we go to Hershey?" he asked.

"That's two hours away," Minette said.

"And it's not on the right highway," Jules replied.

"It's a road trip," Benji replied. "Can't we have a little fun?"

"This is not a vacation," Jules snapped. "I can leave you right here at the bus station and you can take a bus to the airport and fly to California."

"Relax, Jules," Benji said. "Whatever."

And that's how the trip officially began. Jules drove to just about State College, playing chauffeur to his siblings in the back who, after their chicken nuggets and hot apple pies, dozed with their heads against the windows. He paused at the rest stop near exit 147. When the car stopped, Benji and Minette woke. The sun had set, and they all used the bathroom and fed change into the vending machines. Drinks in hand, they all strode toward the picnic tables but didn't sit down, merely walked.

Benji offered to take the next shift. Minette joined him in front. Jules stretched out as much as he could in the backseat and tried to sleep. It must have worked because sometime later he found himself disoriented and surrounded by the strange pseudo-darkness of orange highway lights. Jules shot upright. Minette was asleep with her head against the front passenger window. Benji was not in the car. Jules' senses sharpened. But before he even wiped the sleep-sand from his eyes, he smelled it.

Gas.

He peered out the car and realized Benji must have stopped for fuel. The building beside the Rolls didn't have any branding, no familiar names or logos of petroleum giants. The window closest to them had a faded yellow countertop inside, with what appeared to be a hot dog roller, and in the corner, Jules thought he saw a restroom. He opened the door and straightened his legs. The highway remained frighteningly close, adding the ambient noise of engines and a faint artificial breeze. Beyond this small building, a ramshackle structure that he had a hard time believing had passed health inspections, Jules saw no other structures. Just the deep lines of trees and hills on the horizon. A twenty-year-old pick-up truck had parked in front of the building's garage bay, nose of the truck facing him, no license plate on the battered front bumper, and two men, one about his age, another older, sat inside.

The road beside them was a simple, unlit two-lane. Farm fields waiting for spring bordered the other side. At the end of eye-shot, Jules thought he made out a small house, one-story, cottage-style with an oversized roof implying an upper-level bedroom or attic.

Jules slowly walked to the door. The fluorescent lights inside flickered, but he knew it wasn't "real" but a result of his preternatural senses detecting what the normal human eye could not. He found Benji by the beverage cooler, his arms full of chips all with bizarre names to confirm their unnatural origins or perhaps to prove how fun they were: Funyuns, Cheetos, and Munchos among them.

"I was going to grab a couple Red Bulls for the fridge," Benji said when he noticed Jules.

Jules nodded. His senses would not relax. He surveyed the store. Just a clerk. Just Benji.

"I'm going to grab a coffee," Jules said, "and a Tastykake. That almost looks edible."

He picked up a pale cake with icing that came in packs of three. Butterscotch Krimpet.

"We can share," he said.

He tossed the package into Benji's arms, landing it on top of the chips. Jules went to the coffee pot and poured himself the largest cup they had. He carried it to the clerk. He set it on the counter. He pulled out the corporate card.

"Come on, Benji," Jules goaded.

Benji dropped his pile of snacks beside Jules' coffee. It now contained Slim Jims, sunflower kernels and honey-roasted peanuts among the Red Bull and chips. From a twisty fixture on the counter, Benji snapped off a disposable camera and tossed it beside the snacks.

"Wake Minette so she can use the bathroom," Jules said as he paid the bill and handed Benji the bag. "That's where I'm headed."

Benji also grabbed his coffee. He headed to the car as Jules followed the narrow hallway to the restroom. He did what he needed to do quickly, and met Minette at the door.

"How are you doing?" he asked.

She shrugged and headed into the ladies' room. Jules planned to return to the car, but as he leaned into the door the weight of an unknown gaze struck him. The younger man in the pick-up truck had his head turned and his eyes focused intently on the restrooms. Jules' instinct told him to wait for Min. She came out a moment later, wiping her hands on her thighs.

"They had one of those giant towels, like actual towels that hang out of a dispenser on the wall," she explained.

He touched her elbow and nudged her gently toward the door. She looked at him, a tad confused, but he returned her expression with sternness. She nodded, ever so slightly. The hair raised on the back of his neck.

They left the convenience store. They crept across the parking lot, and Jules felt the stare of the two men in the truck. His muscles twitched, the cortisol flooding his system and urging him to shift. No, he told himself, just walk to the car. He heard Minette swallow and could smell the fear on her.

"I got you," he muttered.

Benji hopped out of the car, holding an enormous peanut butter cup, mouth stained with chocolate.

"Who's driving?" he asked.

"Where did you get that?" Jules snarled.

Benji dropped the candy. The giant Reese's fell to the cement in front of the gas pump and shards of chocolate showered the ground.

"Get in the car," Jules ordered, using the same tone. "I'll drive."

Jules slipped into the driver's seat, Minette at his side up front. Benji ended up in the back.

"What's going on?" Benji asked.

"The men in that truck," Jules said as he shifted the Rolls into gear, "are watching Minette."

"We're in the middle of nowhere," Benji said.

"Exactly," Jules said.

"They could be bored," Benji suggested.

"No," Jules said. "It's predatory."

Jules pulled onto the road and to the entrance ramp. The truck followed. Jules, the quiet chef who spent most of his time denying his wild animal side, did something he had never done before. Not even when he first started to drive. Not even when driving on long, straight desert roads. Not even in Germany.

He pinned the accelerator to the floor. He braced for the car to lurch forward and scream, but the Rolls just gently and silently zoomed as Jules merged into the passing lane. The pick-up truck at first matched them but quickly lagged behind. Jules, attention focused on the rearview mirror, raced ahead. His siblings chattered and ate meat sticks.

He maneuvered the car between some trucks— heavy tractor-trailers moving at a steady pace, one at his left as he settled himself between two in the right lane. Under the protection of the cargo vehicles, Jules blindly took the next exit. The signs indicated they were not too far outside of Clintonville, Pennsylvania.

But Clintonville ended up being nowhere. Just road, with a few sparse lights in the distance indicating the presence of a small town that was currently closed. Jules pulled into the first business he drove by, a Kenworth dealer, and drove into the back of the lot between the cabs for sale. It's not easy to hide a Rolls-Royce but here it might be possible.

"What are we doing?" Benji asked.

"Hoping our friends went home," Jules said.

He sipped his coffee and let the warmth of the cup soothe his hands, and in turn, his nerves.

"How long are we going to sit here?" Benji asked.

"I just need to think," he answered.

"Wouldn't it make more sense to stay on the highway around other people than wherever this is," Minette said.

"Yes," Jules agreed. "But I need a minute."

The heat of his siblings' gaze burned into him. He grabbed the atlas and studied the map of Pennsylvania.

"Well," Jules said, "if they turn up in the next few minutes..."

He paused.

"... would we have to fight them?" he asked.

Benji blanched as his eyes popped from his face.

"I'm going to drink this coffee," Jules said, "and get back on the road."

He reached into the pile of snacks Benji had amassed.

"Where are my crumpets?" he asked.

"You mean krimpets," Minette corrected.

She grabbed the Tastykakes from Benji before Jules could get them. She turned the cakes upside down against her lap and rubbed the cellophane back and forth. She flipped them and started removing the wrapper.

"What was that for?" Jules said.

"The static electricity keeps the icing from sticking," she answered.

"You've done this before," he replied.

"I hang out at the Wawa," she said with a slight smile.

"A Wa-what?" Benji said.

"It's the local convenience store. Pennsylvania's 7-Eleven," she explained as she handed him one of the narrow cakes.

"Oh," he said, accepting it.

She gave Jules his and kept the last.

"*Salut*," she said.

The cake reminded him of a Twinkie in texture, but denser, and the icing tasted like candy. For a brief, still moment, with Benji devouring the krimpet in one bite and Minette gnawing daintily as if Jules had no intention of ever feeding them again, Jules forgot about the nonsense and felt like a kid on a road trip. The three of them hadn't been together like this in years, though two-out-of-three was common, and his parents tried to gather them for holidays.

"This feels good," Jules said softly.

"You can't go wrong with Tastykakes, really," Minette said.

"I'll take your word for that," he added.

He traced the wood accents in the center of the steering wheel.

"When this is over, maybe we should plan a real road trip. Like a weekend getaway," Jules said. "A surfing trip. I've always wanted to catch some waves in Réunion."

"You can't fly down there on a weekend," Benji said.

"Oh shut up," Jules replied. "I wasn't being literal. I just meant I'm enjoying seeing you guys."

"Yeah," Minette said. "We should plan something this summer."

"When golden girl is on her break," Benji remarked.

Minette glared at him. "You need to grow up. Decide what the hell you want to do with your life."

They waited— bickering more than they talked— for nearly an hour. There was no sound and no life among the mammoth trucks. Sleeping mechanical sculptures, rolling workhorses, some with well-furnished mini rooms attached to their booming engines... in some ways a truck would be more practical than this Rolls, Jules thought. And he laughed a little. No one noticed, because his brother and sister were fighting over Funyuns, as if artificial onion circles deserved their dueling.

Minette won the battle, so Jules had the crunching closer to his ear. Benji, in his defeat, retrieved a bag of Cheetos. Jules imagined orange fingerprints across the car's leather interior.

Upon return to the highway, Jules scouted no familiar pick-up trucks. He still had a lingering concern in his gut, and his wolf instinct urging him to run.

Hopefully, the Rolls could run fast enough and he could protect his pack. He watched Benji from the rearview mirror, as his older brother munched on the Cheetos.

Benji had always been perfectly boring and perfectly dependable, skipping college to pursue professional surfing and supporting himself by tending bar. So, it wasn't as if he were a complete liability. He lacked maturity, but he had coordination and physical strength.

Benji crumbled the little bag and tossed it to the floor.

"Excuse me," Jules barked.

Benji froze. He leaned down, retrieved the bag with a crinkle, and placed it in one of the plastic sacks from their frequent pit stops.

"That's better," Jules said.

He gazed to Minette. She still had the Funyuns in her hand, but her head had fallen against the passenger side window and she appeared asleep. Jules quieted his thoughts and focused on her breathing and listened for her heart rate. She wasn't quite slumbering yet, but she was close. Good, he thought. She needed her rest.

By the middle of Ohio, the car had fallen silent and Jules listened to "classic rock" on a radio station that he wasn't sure he liked. Everyone slept until dawn— except for Jules— at which point they stopped at a diner to stretch their legs and have some breakfast. Minette hadn't driven yet and was gearing up to take her turn with lots of hot chocolate, whipped cream dripping down the side of the mug. Jules dipped his finger into it.

"It's real," he remarked.

Minette shrugged. "Makes no difference to me."

They ended up in Fremont, Indiana. Jules had wanted to stop somewhere after Toledo but the options were sparse.

"I feel like everyone is staring at us," Minette said.

Benji put down his fork full of pancakes and turned to look at the other diners at the counter. Jules scanned the room with his eyes. The family wondered if Benji had the werewolf condition, but Jules had no doubt it had skipped him. His brother had no preservation instinct, and acted more like prey than predator. And his sense of smell was lacking. Benji's head refocused to his plate.

"Why are you looking at me like that?" he asked Jules.

"No reason, other than you're a dork," Jules replied, plucking a piece of cut pancake from the plate. "Just promise me..."

Jules dropped the pancake, dripping with cheap table syrup, into his mouth and chewed.

"If I *ever* give you a command, you follow it, without hesitation."

Benji's face scrunched up and he tossed his fingers about flippantly.

"Benjamin-Louis, promise."

He said Benji's name with full French emphasis. Benji tightened his lips, inhaled sharply through his nose, and sighed.

"Fine."

Jules smiled. The grumbling commenced.

"I'm the oldest," Benji reminded him. He aggressively cut more pancake. "And you two think you can push me around like a baby."

Minette leaned closer to him, she was sitting next to Jules in the vinyl booth. "You know—"

"Yeah," Benji snapped. "You guys know what's out there. You guys have seen shit. I'm just a boring person."

"And you act like a child!" Minette returned.

The energy in Minette shifted. Her calmness and fatigue had disappeared. Jules recognized the vibration of aggression her body transmitted. Jules closed his eyes.

"Guys," he said quietly.

CHAPTER FIFTEEN

They rode into Chicago late morning, a little more than three hours after breakfast. Jules had taken over driving again for the last leg. The car handled beautifully but felt ostentatious and large on the highway. It garnered much attention. But among the traffic in downtown Chicago, as they drew closer to Lake Michigan, Jules noticed it seemed to fit in more.

And when they arrived at the hotel, the building covered an entire block and stood far more ostentatious than they did. Even if they were all— Chicago herself, the Peninsula Hotel here and the Rolls Royce—very elegant. In many ways, the Chicago Peninsula mimicked the New York Peninsula, but for some reason even with similar architecture, in Chicago the building looked friendly and warm. Even the stone looked softer. And unlike Manhattan, Chicago did have sunlight which gave the building a welcoming glow. Even if the basic entry looked the same, the experience felt very different.

A valet took the car as another staff member— a white toy soldier just like in New York, the formality of the uniforms in both places struck Jules as dehumanizing and ridiculous— loaded their meager baggage onto a buggy. Minette turned to Jules.

"This is crazy," she said.

"*Ouais*," was all Jules could muster.

The *deja vu* taunted Jules. He hated the pampering the first time. It didn't get easier in a new city.

"Are they here?" Minette whispered.

Jules closed his eyes, inhaled deeply through his nose, and listened for Kait. He might be able to smell Étienne, but it was more likely that he could sense Kait. They had a supernatural connection from the years of service they had shared. He still didn't understand this cosmic werewolf calling and its rules, but her recent fall from grace had relieved him of official duties.

But now Minette had been conscripted into aiding the fire guardian, but as the only female among the werewolves and with the whole system now turned on its own ear, no one knew what was happening anymore and why. The system of magickal balance had broken. Their job— the guardians and the werewolves— was to protect the creative balance of the universe so no single person could become a god.

Six months ago, Kait's brother had proven to be such a threat. Galen had worked for centuries to collect magickal prowess, and in the end, it wasn't Kait nor Jules nor any of the guardians that stopped him. It was Étienne, fueled by pure fury when Galen had killed Adelaide. And the he had almost killed Madame d'Amille, except Basilie had survived the attack, by a thread.

The mistakes Étienne had made while ruled by his emotions, and due to his own ignorance of the supernatural world, had led to chaos, a pregnant Kait now in Chicago with him, and if Basilie was right, an undead Adelaide.

And most disturbing, the lead guardian, Neferkaba, the protector of spiritual magick, the overseer of the guardians of elemental magicks (fire, water, air and earth), had disappeared. After thousands of years.

And his sister had just asked him— were they here?

Jules stood on the sidewalk in Chicago, on a warm but windy, spring day, breathing deeply the scents of the city— car exhaust fumes, the sweetness of the water in Lake Michigan, the richness of humanity, the odors of food— hoping to feel his former boss, Kait.

He focused on the sensation of water, the nearness of the lake, and listened for its rhythm. The water would talk to her just as it did to him.

And he felt it. She was near. And she was worried. Whatever was happening, it had gone very wrong.

"Kait is definitely here. But I can't smell Étienne at this distance," he said.

Benji drew closer. He had been snapping photos of the area. Poor Benji had started this trip believing it would be a brief visit to Paris to visit his brother and deliver a passport to his sister.

"This has been crazy," Benji said.

"Maybe we should send him home," Jules said quietly to Minette.

"Let him see the sights in Chicago," she said. "He's harmless."

"He's helpless," Jules said.

Minette shrugged. Benji climbed the front steps and another staff person greeted him as he hopped into the revolving door.

"Let's check in," Jules said.

A doorman asked his name, Jules complied, and within seconds they were ushered to elevators and whisked to the fifth floor. The check-in area featured a long wooden desk with properly shiny, gold plating, and an obscenely large painting, but Jules didn't really have time to digest it before being sent to the next step of the process. Apparently, the hotel featured contemporary art exhibits, but this felt much more medieval with its weird cross of reverent and foreboding.

The elevator opened and there stood Connor, as his name tag stated, in a more traditional navy blue uniform. He had some materials in hand and a large smile.

Inside the starched suit, Connor seemed soft and young. His pale eyes, which might have been hazel or might have been gray, had more hope in them than he saw in the New York staff. His ginger hair needed a trim, but as expected in the high-class luxury business he had it slicked down and under control.

"Mr. Zweigenbaum," Connor said. "So glad to have you staying with us."

Connor even managed to pronounce his name. So far, the experience of the hotel felt the same as New York, but it also felt entirely new. Madame had booked them in the Lake Suite, as the Peninsula Suite was booked. Étienne's corporate credit card suggested that he was in it.

"Would you like me to alert Monsieur d'Amille that you have arrived?" Connor asked.

Jules ears perked. Perhaps when you pay with the same credit card, privacy issues become less private? The staff thought— and Jules wasn't about to correct them— that they were all traveling together.

"No," Jules said. "I'm just a chef. He doesn't need to be disturbed."

Connor nodded with that slow, sad pace that indicated he understood.

"But," Jules said. "I thought he was using a pseudonym."

"Of course," Connor said with a smile. "I presume Felix is expecting you."

Felix Leiter. The American agent in the James Bond franchise. Madame was right. Étienne was predictable. It shouldn't be hard to convince him to go home.

"It's been a while since we have served him or Moneypenny," Connor said. "So we are happy to assist them now, keeping the media away."

Moneypenny. By name, Moneypenny would be the perfect alias for Basilie. While not a fan of the British 007, Jules knew enough to know that Moneypenny was the secretary that flirted with Bond. Could Kait be Moneypenny? But this man clearly recognized 'Moneypenny,' so it couldn't be Kait. But... it couldn't mean Adelaide really was alive?

"Will there be plans for any group dinners or gatherings?" Connor asked. "I will need an approved guest list."

"Not at this time..." Jules stuttered. "I believe his intentions don't involve guests."

"I'm sorry your suite is not closer to the Peninsula suite. But monsieur has already booked the connecting rooms."

Jules noted his use of French. Minette and Benji looked quite bored.

"Monsieur's suite is located...?" Jules asked.

"On the 18th floor," Connor replied. "Will you need access to the kitchen?"

Jules nodded. Connor slipped behind the massive desk. He pulled out another key card and swiped it through the machine.

"Here you are," he said. "The key to Mr. Leiter's suite. The kitchen may not be as versatile as you'd like."

That was too fucking easy, Jules thought as he accepted the key. Minette grew wide-eyed beside him and she trembled with the desire to snatch it from his hands, he could feel it. Jules gazed over his shoulder with his peripheral vision to find Benji floating down the massive hallway, flanked by topiaries and large enclosed cases.

"We'd like to get settled. We have much to do," Jules said.

Connor again offered a familiar nod.

"Let's get you upstairs," he said.

CHAPTER SIXTEEN

As usual, Madame d'Amille had spared no expense and couched them in luxury. Jules could see why Étienne enjoyed The Peninsula, but at the same time, he wondered why a working-class man would indulge in such a preposterous display of wealth. Jules' siblings stood before the massive windows—essentially a glass wall overlooking Lake Michigan.

"Who knew a lake could be so expansive and majestic?" Minette said quietly, her voice dripping with awe.

Jules turned to the lake, closed his eyes and really listened for the pull of the water. To his surprise, the soothing pattern had more strength and depth than he expected. The wind created waves mimicking ocean tides. After the summer sun had warmed the water, and the cooler autumn air cascaded with that heat, he figured the lake would produce some powerful, cold weather surfing conditions. At the same time, the lake carried a captive stagnancy, trapped by land where it longed to be free. He empathized.

A sudden presence made Jules shudder. He would have said he jumped, but his werewolf senses would not allow that. He turned toward the intruder, knowing it was Kait. Minette did not fare so well, as she turned and screamed.

"Hi," Kait said.

It surprised Jules how well-groomed she was, as Kait, in the throes of her supernatural previous occupation, had never wasted time on mundane tasks like combing her hair or bathing. Her small stature and screaming orange-red hair always made him think of a gnome, but he knew her petite size was not from dwarfism but because she had been plucked from the mortal rhythm of life before puberty. A glimmering water droplet pendant fell upon the soft spot at the base of her neck.

"You still wear the necklace," Jules said.

"Neferkaba tasked me to keep the child safe," she said. "Imperviousness achieves that."

Her hands absentmindedly massaged the small lump of her belly.

"Is Neferkaba dead?" he asked.

Kait nodded. But the nod was sad, her face sinking in remorse.

"Oh, Kait," Jules murmured. "What did you do?"

"Can we sit?" she asked, motioning toward the lush seating amid the tall windows that washed the room with sunlight.

They faced an unbelievable view of Lake Michigan. Minette stood near the window, and just shook and stared.

"I told her about the necklace," Kait said.

Jules had to stifle his rising temper. "Who, Kait? Who killed Neferkaba?"

"I don't know how things got so out of control," she said.

"Where's Etienne?"

"He's here," she said. She wrung her hands with a softness that exuded an air of nervousness, something he had never seen in her. "We have to get him out."

Jules stared at her. "Okay, we can fly back to Paris tomorrow."

She chuckled. And while Kait usually laughed with vivacious abandon, this was a stifled noise of discomfort.

"You haven't realized what we did."

"That's why I'm asking, Kait. What did you do?"

In his mind, he kept repeating one sentence— please don't say what I think you're going to say.

"I helped Etienne resurrect Adelaide,' she said.

Minette gasped.

"How is that even possible?" Jules asked.

"The magick of guardians has unknown potential."

Kait tapped her foot rhythmically on the floor. Silence swallowed them as Jules panicked internally, fighting the desperate urge of his body to transform into a wolf and barge into the suite on the 18th floor.

"She's going to suspect my absence if I stay away much more," Kait said. "I didn't... We couldn't... I didn't know Adelaide had it in her to be evil."

Jules peered deep into her eyes.

"That's a lie," he said. "You have experienced the corruption of the magick."

Kait shrugged, trying to hide the emotional discomfort that Jules could smell.

"I thought she would protect my baby."

Kait mentioned that Adelaide had plans tonight to visit her grave, and that maybe, while she was gone, Jules could rescue Étienne.

"Why is she going to her grave?"

"She goes every night, never for long. She thinks if she does it for a full moon cycle of 28 days it will allow her to ascend to full power."

"Did you tell her that?"

"No," she said, "I just told her that home soil could be powerful. We all have attachment to our roots."

"Then wouldn't she go to her parents' house and not her grave? She's not a vampire."

"You know Adelaide," Kait said. "She's not very bright."

Then she walked out of the room, like an ordinary guest. Minette hadn't even moved from her spot by the window, and Benji had been on the toilet in the nearby powder room the entire visit. Kait had literally wandered into their suite and provided them the 'when' part of their upcoming interaction with Étienne. But she had also confirmed what Jules thought was the worst case scenario.

Étienne d'Amille had resurrected the foolish supermodel. Jules couldn't believe there was any scenario where resurrecting a dead girl would not throw off the delicate balance of the universe. Madame had asked Jules to bring Étienne home, but would he want to come?

"Adelaide's alive?" Minette said. "For real?"

Jules threw his hands in the air. A toilet flushed.

"I don't know."

Benji appeared in the doorway. He looked first to Minette and then focused on Jules who paced around the couch.

"I missed something," Benji said.

"I need to work out a plan," Jules muttered. "Anybody hungry?"

Benji shrugged.

"This is crazy," Minette muttered in response.

"Do you know what Chicago is known for in the culinary world?" Jules asked.

"Deep dish pizza?" Benji replied.

Recognition flashed across Jules' face. "Well, yeah, but there's also hot dogs."

"And you're a pescatarian remember?" Minette remarked.

"There's a Lou Malnati's down toward the Riverwalk," Benji said.

"But they're really good hot dogs," Jules insisted.

Jules wanted to buy hot dogs for his siblings, because a deep dish pizza is not as unique as the Chicago hot dog. These jokers grew up on Book It and Pizza Hut so would they really find deep dish pizza worth the detour? They had to acknowledge their German side and explore the trademark Chicago 'sausage.'

When people heard his name and the ease with which he spoke French, he would often joke that he was half-American with German roots and half-French, so he loved a good hot dog, but he hated himself for it. But he hadn't eaten meat in years. But his siblings possessed the same genetic heritage he did. He could share his former love of mystery salvage meat. And he knew where to find the best hot dogs in Chicago.

How could they want pizza?

So reluctantly, the elder and the younger Zweigenbaum sibling trudged to the car. Jules drove the Rolls out to North Clark Street, following 41 along the lake so they could get char dogs with everything and take them to the beach. The water would center him, and maybe the char dog, with its flesh cooked over the open flame, would mean something to Minette. Jules said something to that extent to Minette, but she didn't find it funny.

The art on the signs and the window decals at Wieners Circle reminded him of classic 1950s tattoos, but with wieners and buns instead of roses, skulls, swords and knives. Benji and Minette sat at the long, red picnic tables while Jules ordered. The sign's red and black plastic letters on the marquis commented about the WMD in Iraq. And for a moment, Jules forget about his six hot dogs and remembered that they weren't the only ones at war.

An employee told him to "step the fuck up" and so he ordered. He got the dogs, some fries and some sides of cheddar sauce. They returned to the Rolls and drove to the North Avenue Beach, where Jules paid too much for parking.

Unrolling the white paper inside the paper boats, they found a long but dark and shriveled beef hot dog— after all Chicago was a slaughter town—snuggled inside a poppyseed bun, smothered with vivid relish, a full quarter slice of dill pickle, mustard, and onion, topped with sliced tomatoes and sport pepper, which looked like anemic jalapenos, and unseen but detectable to his werewolf nose was the celery salt. Minette accepted two hot dogs.

Somehow, Minette convinced him to visit the nearby zoo.

"This isn't a vacation," he remarked.

"No, it's not," she said. "But we could use a chance to relax.'"

Benji ate four hot dogs in about three bites with minimal chewing.

"So after the zoo, can we go for pizza?" Benji asked.

Jules munched on some French fries.

CHAPTER SEVENTEEN

A tired Jules, wondering if this is how their parents felt after outings with them, sat on the couch watching television, waiting for Kait's signal that Adelaide had gone. They all had spots of sunburn on their face.

"I don't understand," Benji said. "How will you know?"

"I'll know," Jules answered.

He had pulled his hair into its regular ponytail, the one he wore while working. He wore a black turtleneck and black jeans and felt more like a cat burglar that a chef.

"But how?" Benji asked again.

"He'll know," Minette said forcefully.

And then he knew. The feeling welled inside of him and provided a pull as clear as if a voice had whispered in his ear.

"Let's go," Jules said.

Minette rose from the couch fluidly and without hesitation. Benji stared, his expression quizzical and yet fixed.

"You just... know."

"Yes," Jules said. "Look, you don't have to come."

"You're not even really involved," Minette said.

Benji shot up, first toward her and then spun toward the windowed corner of the room.

"This whole trip is about me not really being involved," he said. "I was just a better way to deliver your passport."

Minette shrugged. "You could have used an envelope."

"You two never wanted me around," he said.

"That's not true," Jules said.

Boyhood instinct and feelings led Jules to jump into his brother's face. He lifted his pointer finger and pressed it to Benji's chest.

"As soon as we moved to this country, you wanted nothing to do with us."

"Actually," Minette said. "Benji, you always hated me. Even in France."

"You so wanted to be a cool, French kid in California, you had no interest in us."

"To be fair," Minette said, "I don't think either one of you liked me. But Jules, you at least tolerated me."

Jules grabbed the key off the table near the couch and started walking down the entry hall of the suite.

"Let's go," he said. "I don't care who's coming and who's not."

They went to the larger suite and, as promised, when they swiped the key, the door opened. Kait met them and ushered them into the living room, which greatly resembled theirs, and to a door, unique to the Peninsula Suite, that led to a wrap around, private outdoor terrace complete with a dining area. Kait remained in the door, while the Zweigenbaums explored the view, the patio chairs and the outdoor bar.

From his peripheral vision, Jules tracked movement in the living room. It was Étienne, with wet hair, naked, except for a fluffy white towel around his waist. Kait closed the door. The two of them exchanged words, softly so even Jules' werewolf ears could not eavesdrop on the conversation. As Jules stared, he wondered if the man in the living room was Étienne d'Amille. His trademark crazy-mop-of-hair had been shaved short at the sides with only marginal curls on top. And his face presented a chaotic display of uncontrolled beard hair.

Jules grabbed the door, which despite tiny Kait leaning on it, opened easily. Étienne turned toward him, and his expression registered confusion and agitation. As he moved, the swish of the towel revealed a scabby gash on his leg. It looked like someone had reopened the wound from the monster of Ghoubet. It had turned unhealthy shades of green and black and the skin around it seemed swollen, agitated and red.

"Maybe you should put some clothes on," Jules suggested in French.

Étienne disappeared into the depths of the suite. The others came inside as Kait scowled at Jules. For a moment, he thought she might take a swing at him. And he supposed that he would have let her. Without her magick, she wasn't a threat. Without her magick, she resembled an angry toddler.

Étienne returned wearing generic gray sweatpants and a black tee-shirt that said Chicago in screenprinted letters with "est. 1837" in the center. It was like someone had dropped him off at a local Walmart and he emerged with no recollection of who he was.

Jules had no words.

"What is wrong with you?" he finally said.

Étienne merely gestured.

"You leave your wife and your baby and your business," Jules began. "Not to mention those of us scouring the African countryside for you. And you come to Chicago and resurrect a dead girl? Are you an idiot?"

Étienne opened his mouth but before he could speak Kait preemptively interrupted.

"We all know the answer to that."

Benji snickered. Jules shot a cold glance his way.

"I mean, can you even tell me your full name or has this nonsense brainwashed you?" Jules asked.

"Do you even know my full name?" Étienne answered.

"I can Google it," Jules replied.

"Couldn't I?"

"Could you?" Jules retorted.

"Ummm," Minette murmured, gaining confidence as the syllable dragged on. "I agree that this situation makes no sense, but we're working on limiting time. So we need to decide if we're in this together or as adversaries."

"So you don't need my full name?" Étienne asked.

He waved them to the sofa and chairs of the suite's living room.

"For Kait, I will do this in the English," he said. "So please give pardon. She is not well, my cabbage. She is, how to you say... dangerous."

"She has strong magicks swirling in her, what Galen did to her and what Galen taught her about power, it's changed her," Kait said. "And people aren't supposed to come back from the dead. The body isn't made for reanimation. It's like so many of your modern disposable items, one use and in the trash."

"And she killed Neferkaba," Jules added. "Do you two have an end game? What do we do with her?"

"We kill her," Kait said without any hesitation, "before she hurts someone."

Kait peered to Jules and then turned her head to Étienne.

"I will not," Étienne said.

"Why did you resurrect her if you now what to kill her?" Jules asked.

"Hormones?" Kait asked. "What I see now is not what I saw in my head when I started this. I spent 400 years as an immortal with extraordinary gifts. It takes a while to come down from that. You know I was a child when this started, right? When my brother murdered my mother and Neferkaba chose me for this? What were you doing at my age?"

Étienne blushed.

"Did you make mature decisions?"

Etienne chuckled. "No."

"Because here I am— in a new goddamn millennium, illiterate, tiny, pregnant, and my only practical skills are medicinal herbs and midwifery," Kait said. "And now— of all times— I suddenly have the brain of an adult instead of a self-absorbed, thrill-seeking, horny teenager. And Adelaide was the last of my familial line who had the gift. It ends with her. I wasn't ready to accept that."

"You're related to Adelaide?" Jules asked.

Kait nodded. "Cousins about twenty generations removed. I've watched everyone with the gift. And that's not easy. They usually have difficult lives. I thought I could save her."

"Maybe I didn't need saving," a new voice said from the fair side of the room.

Jules turned to face the speaker, which while new to the conversation was certainly known to all of them. The formerly deceased Adelaide Pitney stood before them, dressed in black leather pants that clung to her body like she had an audition for the villain in the upcoming Batman movie. Her cashmere sweater, the color of red wine, didn't hang any looser. And her boots— thigh high black stilettos with hooks, eyes and laces— didn't seem like the appropriate attire for someone frequenting graveyards.

Jules' guts clenched when his eyes met hers. He never denied the obvious aesthetic nature of Adelaide's heart-shaped face, vivid blue eyes and waves of strawberry blond hair. Her lipstick matched her sweater. But he also never liked Adelaide. And now, those same blue eyes, completely surrounded by dark eye shadow, pierced him—no, all of them— from across the room. Her hair billowed over her shoulders much longer than it had been before her death.

"Why are you here?" Adelaide asked. "I have no intention of throwing dinner parties."

"Madame d'Amille asked me to find Monsieur," Jules said.

She strode across the room and into Jules' personal space. Adelaide drew so close to him that her nose practically touched his. Both taller than average, they now stood literally head-to-head.

"You found him, now go."

Her vibes washed over him like a gust from the deep-freeze walk-in. He couldn't sense her heart, or her mood, or the subtle things that made someone... human. She felt... like... like... and as he struggled to put a label on the sensations he realized that it wasn't what she resembled or exuded, but what she no longer had.

Adelaide no longer had doubt, guilt or shame. She was no longer the insecure, pouty child that followed Étienne around the world. She stood tall. She spoke boldly and directly. And that's when Jules figured it out, Adelaide had no emotions. Their breathing synced. Her eyes did not waver from his eyes. The air connected them sizzled with something that felt like static electricity.

"You don't want to challenge me, wolf. Leave here and don't threaten my family."

"Your family?" Jules repeated. His arm flung out toward Étienne. "He has a family! It does not include you. He has a wife, and a son, and even a mother, brother and grandmother!"

Étienne's head tilted. "He is here with you. And maybe he has something to say."

They cheated out to face him, each still keeping a honed eye on the adversary.

"We have need to... how to you say... refuse the situation," Étienne said.

"Diffuse," Jules corrected him.

"Yes," Étienne said as he waved toward Jules. "Adelaide is with us again, and would it not be better to..."

Everyone stared at him.

"We have a responsibility to those we have tamed," Étienne continued in French.

"We're quoting *The Little Prince* now?" Adelaide said. She planted her hands on her hips.

Étienne crossed the room and joined them. He reached for Adelaide, setting the outside of his hand against his cheek.

"Perhaps we have made a mistake," he said, "but I hope we can fix it."

"Are you referring to me as a mistake?" Adelaide replied. "Everything I did for you. Everything I sacrificed for you! All the years I spent trying to show you who I really was and you didn't see me? And I'm a mistake!"

She slapped his hand away, her face reddening and rage oozing from pores. She seized Étienne's wrist, twisted his arm, and pushed him to his knees on the floor.

"I will no longer be anyone's mistake," she said. "That was the story of my life. Everyone wanted the girl in the pictures."

The pressure on Étienne's arm put it in a very awkward position. His heart rate had increased, and before he decided to hold his breath his respirations had sped up as well. His eyes pleaded with Jules, who looked to his siblings and saw shock on their faces. Even Kait looked pale— if one could look pale with more freckles than bare skin. Adelaide didn't say the words, but in action, she had challenged Jules to a duel.

"I know you want me dead," she said, eyes honed on Jules.

You're already dead, bitch, he thought, locking on to her every twitch.

"He's still confused," she continued, referring to Étienne, "but he always refused to believe I was who I was. He had his fantasy."

Jules fell into his preternatural state, where seconds slowed to an eternity and lightning shot through his bones. Jules' face exploded. In their time, it happened nearly instantaneously. He could tell by the widening of his eyes. Minette screamed. But, in his experience, it happened slowly and painfully.

It always started with the jaw, the bones cracking and pushing forward, mouth suddenly filled with fierce teeth. Pain rocketed from the edge of his face into his ear canal as his skull literally broke apart, his body convulsing with fever. In those micro-seconds, the world disappeared as his body somehow rebooted like a malfunctioning computer and re-fired with an entirely new set of code. New default directions normally dormant rewired every cell.

He could feel his bones lengthen and reform. Every nail that broke through his fingertip he experienced one by one. His muscles wrapped around bone in new shapes that made him stronger, fiercer and dangerous, creating an afterburn of the most intense weight-lifting session ever. And the fur, that was the final step. The fever died as the fur coated his skin, and brought a calming sensation like being wrapped in a blanket.

And it happened in under thirty seconds.

Jules, now fully transformed into a majestic timber wolf, honed in on Minette's feral screams. Kait had moved. Étienne still sat trapped by Adelaide. Jules' nose alerted him that Minette had started her change. Next, he focused on the fear wafting from Benji.

And really, Jules thought to himself, his situation did not look good. He was the only normal human in the room not under attack. If anything else went down, he would be the next logical target.

"She's got a butcher's knife!" Benji screamed.

Jules rotated his head and suddenly Adelaide had the blade of a high-carbon, Wüsthof kitchen knife pressed to the front of Étienne's throat, one hand still grasping his arm with a force that suggested she might snap it. Kait rose. She didn't move, leaving the two wolves in between her and Adelaide.

"Adelaide," she said. "Why would you want to hurt Étienne?"

"This is all just crazy!" she bellowed.

"It is," Kait replied. "So, let's think about what our goals are and how we can achieve them."

Kait had her arms out and her fingers splayed, moving as delicately as her awkward body would allow. She started to close the space between them.

"Why are they here?" Adelaide asked. "We have broken the circle of the Guardians so there is no one to assign them to us. Did you call them? Did you betray me?"

"No," Kait said.

"I think…" Benji said tentatively, "that his wife looked up the credit card records."

"She's not his wife," Adelaide spat.

Her grip on Étienne tightened and pain rippled across his face erupting into sweat on his forehead as the knife dipped into his neck.

"She divorced him," Adelaide continued.

"Mon chou, this is an old argument and it doesn't matter how married we are."

Kait closed her eyes as sadness washed over her. Jules understood her despair. Reminding Adelaide of how wrong her perceptions were would not de-escalate her behavior. Jules thought maybe he could sail across the room and knock both Adelaide and Étienne to the floor, and probably successfully pin Adelaide with his front paws while kicking Étienne out of the way with his rear legs. But that led him to ask if she had the reflexes and the basic knowledge of anatomy not to pierce Étienne's jugular in the process.

A few careful steps and now Minette stood opposite him, the two wolves like the highest points of a Y, with Kait in Adelaide's direct path at the base. Together, the two wolves approached Kait, tightening the gap. Minette snarled and snapped her mighty jaw. Minette and Kait seemed to proceed together toward her, so he joined them. Adelaide's eyes flitted between them all.

Adelaide gnarred. The human ear might have taken it as a gesture of fierceness and anger, but Jules knew she had just lost her sense of superiority. Jules knew he only had a nanosecond to take advantage of her insecurity, and so he leaped.

Adelaide released Étienne's arm and shoved him to the floor. She swung the knife at Jules. He did drop her onto her back, but not before the knife sliced him in the chest. His thick mane absorbed most of the blade. Minette blocked the rear, forcing Adelaide tight against Jules as she continued thrashing with the knife. He snatched her wrist with his mouth and when her bones crushed between his teeth, she released the weapon.

Benji ran for Étienne and helped him to his feet. As they retreated toward the couch, Adelaide kicked Jules' flank. The force dislodged his hold. Adelaide gained enough freedom to kick and flail. She sizzled and sparked with magical forces that seeped into Jules' system and short-circuited his body. She tossed him away, and he sailed into the glass between the living room and the private outdoor terrace. It knocked the wind out of him.

Adelaide scrambled to her feet. Minette bound toward her. Minette grabbed the ankle of Adelaide's fancy leather boots and brought her down again. Kait turned to Étienne and pulled him toward the suite's main entrance. Adelaide wouldn't have that. Minette still on her leg, Adelaide lunged toward the pair. She seized Étienne by the ankle, creating a living daisy chain of body parts. As he joined Minette and Adelaide on the floor, Adelaide reached out her free hand and gestured as Jules had seen hundreds of times.

Adelaide opened a travel portal. Adelaide had learned how to slice into the fabric of space and time. Kait's eyes grew wide and she screamed. Jules, shaking off the blow and his wounds, climbed to his feet. As he did, he saw his fleshy hands in front of him. He had transformed back into human form upon impact.

Adelaide dragged Étienne toward her and with unnatural momentum tossed Étienne into the gleaming silver portal. And then, she let go of him. Kait fumbled backwards. She met Jules' eyes and Jules opened his mouth as if to speak but had no words. So, he leaned down and retrieved the knife that Adelaide had dropped.

"Let her go," Kait screamed to Minette.

Minette opened her jaws. Kait raced toward the portal, laced her fingers into Adelaide's hair, and dove into the silver light as the portal began to close. Blood spattered Jules' chest. Minette's wolf form rolled and convulsed as the adrenaline left her system and her body involuntarily returned to human form. The knife still in his left hand, Jules offered his sister assistance with his right. He pulled her up, the two of them standing naked before their older brother.

"For the record," Jules said, holding up the blade, "this is a fillet knife."

"Good to know," Benji said quietly.

CHAPTER EIGHTEEN

"What to do we now?" Benji asked Jules.

They had clothed and reassembled in the living area of their room. Jules called Madame and reported what had happened. He confirmed that Adelaide was indeed alive, and that she had escaped with Étienne after a pretty intense fight.

Jules didn't mention that Adelaide had sliced the space/time continuum, which exponentially expanded the possibilities of where they could be, and that Étienne had entered alone, which might have killed him, because mortal bodies couldn't withstand the experience. And if he had survived, he might have traveled somewhere completely separate from Adelaide and Kait. Anywhere in space or time.

So, that sucked. Jules sat on the couch, elbows on his knees, running his fingers threw his hair. He tried to explain everything to his siblings, but he didn't really know much about it. And it felt like the more he talked, the less things made sense.

"How do the portals work?" Minette asked.

Jules shrugged. "The being that opens them directs them. That's all I know."

"Okay," Minette said.

She sat cross-legged on the floor. She placed her hands on the coffee table.

"I'm no physicist," Minette said, "but I know some basic engineering. Circuits, electricity, energy, magick... it's all about harnessing and controlling power."

"Okay," Jules replied, pausing from him from his neurotic hair smoothing.

"If you don't understand it, neither does Adelaide," she said. "You have five years of a head start? Six? What would Adelaide have been thinking when she opened that portal? Is that where Étienne would end up? And would Kait be able to catch him?"

"We need help," Jules said. "And you should both go home. This isn't your fight."

"Should I mix us some drinks?" Benji asked.

Jules chuckled. "Yeah, why not?"

Minette raised her finger. "For one, I'm not twenty-one for another six months."

Benji shrugged.

"But you're still French," Benji said.

Jules rose, and went to his sister who had collapsed into a cozy armchair, patting her shoulder.

"Benji will show us his bartending magic that he uses back-home and we'll rest. Let's take a day or two to focus on you, Min."

"Why me?"

Benji had already disappeared to the ice machine. Jules crouched in front of Minette.

"I don't know why or how you're a werewolf," he said. "But I'm going to make sure you know everything I know. And then we should tell Dad, together."

Minette said nothing.

"And if I were you," Jules added. "I would find an internship for this summer. Give Dad a week or two to poke and prod at you, because we need his knowledge, and then get the hell out of there."

Benji returned with three very purple cocktails on a silver tray.

"Margaritas," he announced.

"Purple?" Jules said, as he stood and accepted one from the tray.

"I added Chambord," he said.

Minette had already brought the glass to her lips. "Oh, that's sweet."

"Raspberry margaritas?" Jules said.

He sipped. The flavor profile was smooth and fruity.

"This is a California drink," Jules decided.

Benji placed the tray on the coffee table and lifted his glass.

"*Santé*," he said, tipping his drink toward them.

"*Santé*," they replied in unison.

The siblings touched glasses, a reverberating clink dancing around the room.

"I wish us all luck," Jules whispered.

Benji finished his margarita first and returned the glass to the tray.

"Thank you, guys," he said. "You didn't have to keep me with you, but you did. And despite risking my life, I've enjoyed it."

"So you don't mind if I drive you to O'Hare tomorrow and put you on a plane?" Jules asked.

Benji shook his head. "I heard what you said to Minette, and you're right. She needs you."

"That's mature of you," Jules said.

"Shut up, asshole," Benji replied with a smile.

"That's my brother," Jules returned, also smiling.

They hugged. The next morning, because they all needed to sleep off what had happened (and split a Chicago-style pizza), Jules and Minette drove Benji to the airport. At the departure terminals, Benji gave Minette a hug and Jules a slap on the arm.

"This was fun," he said. "Weird shit. But nice to spend some time with the two of you. It's been too long."

Jules gave a soft nod. Minette hugged him again.

"Next time," Benji said as he grabbed the handle on the suitcase, "you're coming to my place and we're drinking a lot and surfing on the days we're not hung over."

Jules laughed, surprised but not surprised by the suggestion. It was a great invitation.

"Thank you for your help," Jules said.

"I got in the way," Benji said, "but thank you for not sending me home earlier."

"Sometimes, it feels good to have something normal as an anchor," Jules replied.

Minette gazed at both of them.

"That's why you brought him?" Minette asked.

Jules nodded. "Moral support. And Min, you didn't need to be here either."

He tousled the back of her hair and she flinched. Cars around them outside the terminal honked. Jules could hear swearing in the distance, but it was his supernatural ears doing the listening.

"I have to go," Benji said, checking an imaginary watch. "But I'm looking forward to my first class seats. I've never flown first class before."

Benji departed, disappearing behind the glass and into the crowd.

"It was good to see him," Minette said.

"And keeping him with us prevent *Maman* and Dad from being suspicious," Jules said.

They got back into the Rolls.

"Come on," Minette said. "You liked seeing him."

"Maybe," Jules said, pulling into traffic, "but then I remembered how annoying he is. He's the oldest, but he's so shallow."

"Did you ever think that you're too sullen and serious and judgmental?"

"*Aielle*, Min."

"Yeah," Minette said with a hearty sigh. "Why couldn't have I had a sister?"

They returned to the hotel, planning to give themselves another day to regroup before heading east. They could have long talks in the car about his experiences as a werewolf, his time in Djibouti, what he and Jacqueline had discovered about the medical and genetic factors of lycanthropy, and how he took care of himself.

And he knew he should bait her.

As in, deliberately take his sister somewhere private and incite her to anger or prey on her fears to prompt a change.

And he hated the thought. It twisted his insides as if he needed to use the toilet.

He was always the big brother who protected her and looked after her.

He had a duty to help her hone and control her predator instincts.

And then they had to tell Dad.

"What's wrong?" Minette asked.

Jules' response was monosyllabic.

"You made a strange groan," she observed, "and you feel different. Heavier."

"You realize that's a wolf thing?" he replied. "You tapped into my energy and my body language. I don't think I made a noise."

CHAPTER NINETEEN

"It's a shame we're not into cars," Jules said. "The people at the hotel told me that South Bend, Indiana, was the home of Studebaker."

"Yup," Minette replied. "I don't care. Isn't Notre Dame in South Bend?"

Jules shrugged. Youngstown, Ohio, sat approximately at the midpoint of their journey back to Minette's school. But they only made it as far as Elyria before the Rolls needed gas. Grumbling tummies and the pull of Lake Erie seduced Jules out of the car for a break.

"What's wrong?" Minette asked.

Jules shook his head. "Nothing. I just feel the lake growing farther away. And she is missing to me."

Minette chuckled. "The lake is a she? And you used French syntax in your English."

"Did I?"

Jules grabbed the company credit card and went to the gas pump. After he swiped it, he tapped on Minette's window and she opened the door. He handed her the card.

"Do we need snacks?" he asked.

Unlike when he sent Benji into the mini-mart, Minette returned with sandwiches, coffee and half-pints of chocolate milk. She stocked the fridge with the milk.

"So, these aren't my favorite selections," she reported, "but do you think the vegetarian thing makes a difference?"

She handed him four sandwiches: two peanut butter and grape jelly on wheat, an egg salad on pumpernickel, and a tuna salad on rye.

"Pescatarian," he corrected her, pointing to the tuna sandwich.

She nodded. Jules took the receipt from the gas pump. They both returned to the car.

"Sometimes when I eat meat, the way I tear into it, I can feel the wolf. And when I'm human, I want to be fully human, you know?" he explained. "He's the predator, not me."

He accepted one of the peanut butter and jelly sandwiches and the egg salad.

"If I remember correctly, you don't like egg salad," he said.

"Nope," she said, visibly relieved as she unwrapped the tuna. "Had you taken the tuna, I would have slipped the egg salad in the fridge and survived on the PB&J."

He restarted the car.

"Say your goodbyes to Lake Erie," she said.

"We're inland now. She's already gone."

The radio played classic rock and referred to the alternative bands he had enjoyed a decade earlier as 90s punk. The egg salad used minimal seasonings and therefore bored his taste buds, but the protein and fat would tide him.

"Something similar happens to me," Minette said.

Jules waited for her to continue. She didn't.

"Meat?" he guessed.

"Fire," she replied. "It's only been recent, like maybe a month. But if someone lights a cigarette or there's a candle somewhere in the dorm, I can feel it."

"I don't know how it works for you," he said. "But...the shift... it has something to do with adrenaline and testosterone."

"So you think the excess testosterone in my system is from the transformation or that it caused the switch?" she asked.

They had returned to Route 80 eastbound.

"I don't think the wolf would change your biochemistry," he replied. "Your body overproducing testosterone probably triggered the gene. Maybe all women can be werewolves, they just lack the testosterone to do it."

"That sounds too simple," Minette said.

"Dad said I had to take the medication because adrenaline and arousal would bring it on, so any time I was threatened or scared—"

"Or horny?" Minette interrupted. "That never happened to you, did it? Making out with a girl and—"

"Have you forgotten Laura Portersmith?"

"Oh my God," Minette gasped. "Is that what happened that night? Wow."

"Yeah," he said. "So I did as he said and I took the medication. She triggered my first change."

"Oh."

Minette sat silently, but Jules could feel her thoughts from across the car. He couldn't read them, but he could certainly sense the depth of the contemplation.

"I was pissed, when I first changed," she said. "School was hard, you know? And my favorite class last fall was Earth and Planetary Materials. It was a geology course, so it was nice not to be discussing the environment and water resources. Maybe I picked the wrong major. Maybe I should study volcanoes or something."

Jules smiled at her. With everything that was happening, she hadn't told him exactly when or how she had transformed the first time.

"Juan picked me up at the airport," she said. "And I was so happy to be home, I guess I didn't notice things were off. It felt good to be touched. It felt good to be in California again and away from the East Coast winter."

"Yeah, I never understood the appeal of snow," he said.

"Juan and I have a pretty standard New Year's Eve thing," she said. "We get snacks at 7-Eleven, play video games until the ball drops in New York and then we drive out to the beach, build a fire and cuddle and talk until midnight."

"What happened this year?"

"We went for a walk around the neighborhood, past our old school, and before we even made it to 7-Eleven, he broke up with me."

"And that's when it happened?" Jules asked.

She nodded. "I was heartbroken, and the only word that does it justice is raw."

Minette's face turned red as she spoke about it.

"I ran," she said. "I don't think I've ever run so fast in my life. Juan called to me, but I kept running."

"Did he find you?"

She shook her head. "I stumbled, and at first I thought there had been a rock or a root. My bones were tingling before I hit the ground. It felt like my center of gravity just dropped. There I was, on all fours, howling. I recognized my own voice, but the sound clearly came from an animal."

"Why didn't you call me?"

She shrugged. "I did that thing where I rationalized it. I thought I couldn't be a werewolf, because Dad said so, and maybe in my distress, I fell in the woods, passed out and dreamt the whole thing."

"But then Jaing showed up."

Minette nodded. She finished eating her sandwich. The radio played Green Day. They didn't talk much until they hit the border of Pennsylvania. As they entered deeper into the state, Jules could feel the increase in wildlife and tree density, while he sensed a decrease in human scent, ambient light and man-made pollutants. He gazed to his sister, who seemed to have lost herself in whatever she was pondering as she looked out the window.

"Did you want to drive?" he asked.

"If you need a break, I'd be happy to take over."

"I didn't know if you were bored."

"Not really," she said. "This isn't the most thrilling part of the trip, but it's okay."

And then— amid the stillness of the trees fighting to bear their spring blossoms on oversized purple hills—Jules sensed an unusual life force. He pulled off the next exit, one with no advertised services, hotels or restaurants. The life force had presence more than the local wildlife, a hint of reverberation of the supernatural, but something exotic that pinged in his nose like the right pinch of cinnamon or the luxurious draw of a rose. Or the smell of fresh baked chocolate chip cookies. Even if you're not a fan of the American classic, you can't resist the gooey, warm blend of textures.

"Why are we heading to nowhere?" Minette asked.

They turned left at the end of the long exit ramp.

"I don't know," Jules said.

"Adelaide into rustic camping?"

Jules released a hearty laugh.

"Adelaide is never further than the next Diet Coke-dispensing vending machine. Or *tabac*."

"Adelaide smoked?"

Jules gazed to his sister. The tone in her voice suggested a heavy disappointment.

"Models live on nicotine and caffeine, until they hit the big leagues and go for the cocaine."

"I know but..." Minette's face fell. "Adelaide was so wholesome."

"That's why she had quit smoking and never progressed to cocaine. Don't tell anyone but she had gained ten pounds over the years after she quit cigarettes, and that's why she stopped getting invites for the other big shows."

Minette semi-sighed as she processed this information.

"She seemed like such a role model. She was gorgeous, and sweet, and she worked for Étienne so she didn't hustle like the other girls. I was never really into fashion, but the media made a big deal out of her when she made an appearance somewhere other than Chez d'Amille."

Jules nodded.

"That was all Basilie," Jules explained. "Adelaide was so young, barely a teenager. Right after the big eighties names. Her body resembles theirs. At a time when ultra-skinny came in. So Basilie made her exclusive to Chez d'Amille. She couldn't do anything without permission."

"So she was a commodity?" Minette asked.

"Aren't they all?" Jules replied. "I almost turned Basilie down when she offered me a job."

"What changed your mind?"

Jules chortled. "Kait. Let's face it, that job offer wasn't coincidence. It didn't suck me into this life. I was already in it. But even so, Étienne is a good guy."

They sat quietly as they drove down a pristine country road.

CHAPTER TWENTY

They discovered a small grove with a gravel-lined square that resembled a parking area, no picnic table, no signs, no disturbances at all except a clear trail right smack dab in the middle. Jules stretched his long legs as he opened the car door.

"You have got to be kidding," Minette remarked.

Jules looked over his shoulder and tossed his right hand back in a strangely flamboyant gesture.

"This is how it goes sometimes."

He brought a deep breath of the forest air into his body.

"We don't have much time. It smells like rain."

They walked into the woods, which perhaps with this depth and terrain was more accurately a forest. The forests here in Pennsylvania weren't like the Redwoods in California or the palm trees at the coast, but thick and crowded and overgrown. What typically would be alive with deep variegation of every hue now burst with delicate greens and the dehydrated crispness of leaves and dead underbrush. They had reached that time of the year when the tiny, vibrant plants pushed through their protective blanket of past living predecessors, when trees had buds and sparse leaves as they rebuilt themselves.

"Jules," Minette said.

Jules could smell the new life and the decay. The decay merely resembled the natural layers of the forest in scent, but the newborn plants, they smelled hopeful, like a little bit flower and a tiny pinch of scallion to keep it sassy.

"We're not on the trail anymore."

Jules also smelled the animal. It wasn't local. The regular floral and fauna of a region blended together to form one overarching smell.

"Jules," Minette interrupted again. "Will we be able to get back?"

He ignored the crack in her vocal steadiness. Something in the environment didn't share the same signature. Something was from out of town. And while it smelled of animal, it also smelled human. Minette paused and stared at the sky.

"Jules," she said. "When did it get dark?"

The hairs on the back of his neck stood up, but he wasn't sure they were the human hairs. Jules released his attention from the scent he was tracking.

"Minette, will you stop?!" Jules snarled at her.

She flinched, moving away from him.

"Sorry," Jules said. He took a minute to breathe.

Minette waited.

"I think I felt a raindrop," she said in a mousy voice.

The way she observed him, he could tell she had never seen him quite this... focused.

"Look," Jules said. "There's this zone, where you can use your wolf skills as a human. So I can trace our own scent back to the car. Actually, so can you. Come here and smell me. Smell us. Really smell."

She came closer. She obeyed his suggestion with a deep inhale that filled her entire chest and diaphragm.

"Again," he directed.

And she obeyed.

"Now," he said. "Turn around. Close your eyes. And walk toward that smell."

She almost rolled her eyes at him. Everything about her body language— the low shoulders, the tilted torso and of course the smug mouth— said she didn't believe him. But she did what he asked. She pivoted, apparently she had closed her eyes too soon, and walked right into him.

"Try again," he said. "This time, remember to find the lighter version of the scent."

And this time, he watched her flawlessly retrace their steps for about ten feet.

"That's enough," he said.

Unexpectedly, she spun, and with eyes still clenched tightly, walked fluidly and directly back to him and stopped six inches from him. Her eyes popped open.

"Holy shit," she exclaimed.

She scanned the area around her.

"I could smell it all so clearly, and when I approached you... there was this vibration and heat. And then I could hear your heartbeat. That's when I knew to stop."

"You thought the werewolf gene was just a scary inconvenience? It comes with superpowers."

Minette smiled. For the first time on their hour-plus-long hike she seemed relaxed. Then she noticed something on the horizon. Jules turned and looked in the same direction she did.

"Jules," she said. "Is that the full moon?"

"That's a total myth," he said.

She froze. Her nostrils wiggled as she inhaled.

"I think I smell it," she said. "I smell what you're tracking."

Jules tilted his head in the direction of the scent. Minette led. They moved deeper into the forest, the trees growing thicker and taller as they pushed beyond the trail. In the distance, something trotted through dead leaves, sending a crunch through the forest. The way the sound carried indicated it was a larger animal, probably a deer, potentially a bear. But it did not exist in the same trajectory as their mystery animal. Jules gently touched Minette's shoulder. She stopped. Jules held his hands up. Minette gave a small nod of the chin. She understood his suggestion to wait and listen.

As they observed with their nose and their ears, the scent of the animal they were tracking and the trotting of the mundane critter approached one another. The scent grew stronger and came toward them, and Jules noticed no change in the wind to explain this so the creature had moved directly into their path. The other animal had not noticed it, or if it had it hadn't changed its path or speed.

Minette seemed calm. Her heart rate was stable and her body stood completely still. She was concentrating deeply, which slowed everything about her. His heart, on the other hand, raced— because he suspected that the strange animal was a predator about to launch itself on its prey, whatever was trotting about the woods.

A squeal of surprise. A primal death scream that shook the forest. A clatter and what felt like a large boom. Minette paled and wavered from her still and steady pose. She gasped.

Jules moved ahead of her. He followed the sound of the scuffle and the continued rustle. It was eating. It was hungry. They had no reason to be involved, but he could not turn away now. His own instinct drove him deeper into the forest with Minette, more silent than Jules had expected, close to him.

He held his arm out and stopped her. An obscenely large cat tore apart a young deer. Hunched over the fresh corpse, Jules could not fully determine the predator's body shape or size. It had the sleek, short fur, the angled skull and the muscle lines of a cat. It had some sort of dark pattern, like a leopard's spots. Whatever it was, it had not noticed them. It dug its snout deep into the belly of the deer and devoured its innards.

Clouds almost as dark as the night rolled across the moon. The sky released a deluge of cold rain that immediately soaked them and every scent around them.

"Fuck," Jules muttered.

"It's only water," Minette said. "I thought you liked water."

Jules sighed. "I do, when it's not washing our away our trail back to the car."

"Oh," Minette said.

She surveyed her surroundings.

"Fuck," she repeated.

She returned her attention to the cat eating the deer. Her lips gave an awkward twist and she tilted her head quizzically.

"Jules? Am I seeing things?"

As the rain pelted them, soaked their clothes and drove a chill into their bones, it had also covered the predator. Jules turned in its direction. The rain washed the mutilated carcass and returned its blood and loose bits to the undergrowth and soil. But cat appeared to have gone, not a shock since cats don't like water, but Jules had not heard it depart. And he should have. And next to the deer laid a naked man.

"Depends," he replied. "You don't see a naked man, do you?"

"I do," Minette said.

"A rational person would say he had to have been there all along. That the cat had our attention."

"I'm a twenty-year-old female," Minette replied. "I think I would have noticed the naked man."

Neither of them moved or spoke.

"Should we go check if he needs help?"

Jules gave her his most practiced sibling look of "Are you a complete idiot?"

"Because is there any reason why a naked man lying on the ground deep in the forest wouldn't need help?" Jules replied.

"He might be dead," she said, with a tone that indicated death was a better option than the alternatives.

They crept toward the bodies. And despite the pouring down rain, the smell of death, blood, deer and cat surrounded the scene. Jules knelt beside the man, whose skin tone and dark hair suggested Latin American descent. The rain left his body clean and scent-free, so Jules lowered his nose to the man's mouth. He shuddered.

It smelled of deer flesh.

"This is crazy," he said.

"What?" Minette asked.

"You know what I'm going to say, right?"

"I hope not," she said, her arms crossed and hugging her body, perhaps to fight a chill, perhaps to soothe her nerves.

"Good news is," Jules began, "he's alive and unhurt."

"Bad news?" Minette asked.

"He's the cat."

CHAPTER TWENTY ONE

With no way to find their way back to the car, Jules and Minette stayed with the naked man. Jules would have preferred to think they would have stayed with him even without the rain, but under the circumstances, he couldn't say for sure. The unknown fellow groggily twisted in the grass and rose to his feet, more confused than embarrassed when he woke to found himself, nude, amid the Zweigenbaum siblings in the rain beside a dead deer.

The look that passed between the two men clearly seemed to include a sense of recognition. The man uttered a monosyllabic grunt.

"Um, hi," he said to Jules.

"Yeah," Jules replied. "Hi."

"I don't know what happened," the man said, gesturing toward the deer, "but these woods aren't safe."

"We saw you," Minette said, "with that deer."

"It's okay," Jules quickly said. "It looked like you were hungry."

"Hungry?" the man repeated.

"Maybe not you... exactly as you are now... you," Minette said.

Jules surveyed every inch of the man. His posture and muscle stance indicated preparation for defense, which he supposed his did, too.

"Not safe... because of you?" Jules asked.

"I'm not the only threat," he said.

"I tracked you," Jules said. "I don't know who or what you are, but..."

The man chuckled uneasily. "Look, Buddy. That makes two of us, and if you don't mind, I would rather get out of here."

He turned and took a long, confident stride forward. Jules grabbed his shoulder.

"Were you tracking us?" Jules asked the man.

"No," he said. "I don't know you."

The man successfully left Jules' grasp. Minette jogged after him.

"You're a shapeshifter," she said, "and you turn into this massive cat."

"I don't know who the two of you are," he replied, not even pausing, "but I'm naked and cold."

"We come from a family of werewolves," Minette continued. "We're werewolves."

The man stopped but did not turn.

"A family of werewolves," he repeated.

Jules walked toward Minette.

"My dad says it's a genetic anomaly, but my experience," Jules paused, because he didn't know if he should be quite so honest with a random naked guy in the forest during a full moon, "is that our line may have been bred for supernatural purposes."

Minette pivoted harshly. "Is that what you think?"

Jules thought for a moment. He had never put those thoughts into succinct words before, but yes, he had come to that conclusion. Jules nodded.

"How else do you explain how out of all the people in the world, we both get tied up in an elite circle of five magickal beings?"

"Genetic anomaly... werewolves..." the man muttered. "I'm still naked. And cold."

The man continued walking, and Minette continued following, so Jules had no choice but to join them. They came to a small cabin, a one-room structure that might have been the size of a studio apartment. And Jules was certainly no carpenter but it looked like it had been built out of pallet wood. Neither the exterior nor the interior had been painted. When the man opened the door, not unlocked, just opened, it revealed a single room with a cot mattress, a sleeping bag, a neatly folded pile of clothes, a camping lantern, a flashlight, some paperback books, a box of saltines, a jar of peanuts and a bag of apples. The man went to the pile of clothes and donned pants. Then, he layered on a t-shirt, a flannel and a sweatshirt. A heavy coat hung on the back of the door.

"I can't offer you a chair," he said. "But it's dry."

Minette nodded. The man lit the lantern.

"You saw me," the man said, "and I was a cat."

They both nodded. The man paced the small space.

"And you're both werewolves," he said.

"You seem confused more than surprised," Jules observed.

"How did you get here?" the man asked.

"We were driving through," Jules answered.

"And you just stopped?"

Jules nodded. "Look, I know this sounds strange—"

"Do you have any idea what has happened to me?" the man interrupted.

Jules shook his head. The man sighed and reached for the box of saltines.

"It's been about eight months," he replied. "I woke up in the woods, no idea where I was or how I got there. I had an envelope with some cash, but no wallet. As I started hiking out of the woods, I realized I had no idea who I was. I had no memory."

Jules had no idea what to say. He looked to Minette who seemed sadly transfixed on the man.

"I made it to town, and somehow made it to the hospital," he continued. "They called me John Doe and couldn't find any record of who I might be. They tested me, and other than being a little dehydrated, I was fine. They fed me and let me go, but the town's so small it doesn't have any social services. So, I went to the ice cream shop. The townspeople call me Sweets because I always stop at the ice cream shop."

"I'm Minette, and this is my brother, Jules."

"And you really saw it?"

"The cat?" Minette said. "Yeah."

"I originally came back out here to try and find out what happened to me. Did I have a car? A campsite? I bought a sleeping bag..."

He pointed to the one on top of the cot mattress.

"... and I thought I would keep wandering until I found some trace of... me."

He paused.

"I should have bought a bus ticket to Pittsburgh and found a good social worker."

"Why are you still out here?" Minette asked.

"Because I kept waking up naked in the middle of the forest and the more it happened, the more I remembered tearing animals apart."

He munched on a saltine and offered them the box. Jules refused.

"Salt cleanses the mouth," Sweets said. "Raw deer tastes nasty."

They stared at each other silently while Sweets chewed.

"So I'm a cat?" he said 'cat' as if the word were vulgar.

"You believe us?" Jules asked.

"I smell something on you, and it's not human."

Jules had the suspicion Sweets wasn't being completely honest. But Jules also knew Sweets had good reason not to trust them. Jules had no intention of telling him more than necessary. But, was any of this necessary? And had Jules and Minette already said too much?

"You warned us that the woods are dangerous," Jules said. "What did you mean?"

"There's a killer out here," Sweets said. "And I'm not sure if it's me. I don't think it is, because the bodies aren't eaten. When I wake up near my carcasses, it's obvious I killed to eat."

"You didn't kill us," Minette said.

"Maybe I didn't have the chance," he answered.

The small shack went silent.

"There are soldiers in the woods," Sweets said. "The townspeople say that they came into the woods after the murders. This is all National Forest land. But I found one of the first bodies, and it was a soldier. And I don't think the public ever found out about it. And there's some weird redneck vigilantes, they come out here looking for something."

Jules remembered the men in the pick-up truck that followed them from the gas station on their way to Chicago.

"That's what I know," Sweets said. "I think maybe it's your turn."

Jules looked to Minette. Minette gave a shrug.

"Our family has a long line of werewolves. We were driving to Chicago and we think some men in a pick-up truck were following us the last time we came through here," Jules said. "Now we're on our way back. We came in from a small parking area not too far from Route 80," Jules said. "I think the rain has washed away our scent, so we could use some help finding our car. If you need some clean shirts, I have a few with me."

"You didn't offer me a ride back to civilization," Sweets answered. "You don't trust me?"

"*Au contraire*," Jules replied. "I hate the idea of leaving you here, but from your body language I get the idea that you're not ready to leave."

The pattern of the rain on the roof had lessened. It would stop soon.

"I've never heard of a were-cat," Jules said. "But I also don't know much about werewolves."

"Tell me what you know," Sweets requested.

"It's a recessive genetic trait. Parents carry chimera DNA, DNA of both human and wolf. And the right mix of testosterone and adrenaline activates a switch between human and animal," Jules summarized. "My father is a genetic researcher, specifically in hereditary disorders, and he believed sexual hormones precipitated the change, but for me, it was the stress of a big move and a fight at school."

"And you?" Sweets asked Minette.

"Girls are supposed to be carriers, not shifters," she said. "But a couple months ago, when my boyfriend dumped me, I turned into a wolf. Preliminary tests show that I produce excess testosterone, for a girl."

"So werewolves are real," Sweets said.

"Yeah," Minette said.

"Nothing bit either one of you," he remarked.

"Did something bite you?" Jules asked.

"I found no evidence of anything," Sweets said. "I also wonder if maybe I'm left from some government experiment. These woods are full of soldiers looking for something, doing something."

"We can help you," Minette said.

"But you can't," he said. "I think I was supposed to help you."

Sweets looked deep into Jules' eyes.

"You knew this world was far more complex than you'd been led to believe," Sweets said.

He gestured to himself and then to Minette.

"We're your proof," he said. "She's not supposed to be what she is. You can't feel it, because she's your sister. But I can. Her heart rate, her respirations..."

Jules worked to clear his mind and listen to what this stranger might have heard. He thought about the tests Jacqueline had done in Paris; there was nothing wrong with Minette. And then he thought he heard something. It was so small, he really had to focus. Not small, slight. Something about the pattern of her body's system sounded off, like it had sped up by the tiniest fraction. Minette's eyes grew wide and her lips fell apart like she wanted to speak, or maybe cry.

"Guys," she said.

"Ca va, Minette," Jules told her. "It's okay."

"Is it though?" Sweets said as he opened the door. He led them from the makeshift cabin into the darkness. "My guess? Her body, and the reason biological females do not shift, cannot handle it. The disorder will cause her to prematurely age."

"Guys," Minette said.

The clouds obscured the moon.

"It's a guess," Sweets said as he wove through the trees. "Women's bodies are designed to grow new life, and as such, they divert their own nutrition to offspring during gestation. Their hormone balances are geared toward this as well, so they don't have the same predisposition to build muscle and strength as a male does. And it feels to me like this masculine trait keeps your body from self-destructing because it can recover easier. I think her body surrenders to it, as it would a growing fetus."

"Guys!"

Minette gazed to Jules. As if he knew if Sweets were right. No one knew. But he could certainly share the theory with Jacqueline. But if Minette were in danger, they had to tell Dad.

"Guys!" Minette shouted. "He's a doctor."

She pointed to Sweets.

"How do you know that?" he asked her.

"Listen to all that stuff you just said," she said.

That's when Sweets cocked his head, tilting his ear toward something. He stopped walking. Jules and Minette stopped walking. Jules felt something— definitely a presence, multiple people, not too far. The distant smell of unwashed men, tobacco and cheap liquor carried on the breeze. Sweets made eye contact with Jules with a subtle movement of his head. Jules gave a partial nod. Minette stood between them, eyes wide and heart beating faster, not sure what they had noticed.

If malice had an odor, this would be it.

CHAPTER TWENTY TWO

Five men slowly crept from behind various trees, a mix of flannel, denim and Carhartt. They held guns, long guns with ornately-carved shoulder butts. It was in that moment Jules realized his inexperience and naïveté regarding guns, which one might have thought would have been more obvious since he just returned from a military base. But these weren't soldiers, and the only term he could think of for these dirty men with various levels of scruffy faces was 'rag-tag,' a term he'd always liked since he'd first heard it as a child who had just moved to the United States but never had a chance to use.

"Jules," Minette whispered. "Earth to Jules."

She had raised her hands, as did Sweets. Jules was the only one in a relaxed posture. The guns, and the men, pointed toward Minette.

"She's coming with us," the one in the center said.

He certainly had the most confidence of the group, steadiest heart, straightest posture.

"Like hell she is," Jules replied.

All the men stepped forward, guns pointed specifically on Jules. Minette squeaked.

"That's my sister," he said.

"She's the mother of the anti-Christ," the leader said.

"She's what?" Jules said.

"Great," Minette said. "I've gone from little sister, to mutant, to mother of the anti-Christ."

Jules looked to Minette, whiz-kid of Super Mario Brothers and expert on My Little Pony. The girl probably still bitter that their parents wouldn't buy her a horse. And who still asked clerks at the ice cream shop if the bubble gum ice cream had gumballs in it, because she likes to store them in her cheek and chew them once the ice cream was gone.

"There's an unholy child conceived and it's the spawn of the devil."

Jules sighed. He didn't mean to, but it certainly sounded like these guys had Minette mixed up with Kait.

"I don't know about devil spawn," Jules said. "But…"

Especially since Kait's child had an earthly father— Etienne. And he could attest to that, having witnessed and interrupted the whole exchange. He pondered the idea of Satan posing as Étienne, or that Étienne might actually be the devil. Jules studied the men. The one on the left was one of the men who had followed Minette at the gas station last week.

Shit. The more this made sense, the less it made sense. Sweets raised his eyebrows in Jules' direction.

"It sounds like you almost know what these knuckleheads are talking about," Sweets said.

Jules pointed to the familiar face. "You."

He gestured to Minette.

"You followed us from the gas station last week."

Recognition washed over Minette's face.

"So I'm right," Jules said quietly. "You know the face."

"Fancy car," the man on the left said.

He spit a dark, pungent burst of tobacco chew waste to the ground— and Jules blinked hard to confirm he hadn't just imagined the stereotypical behavior. He could not wait to leave Pennsylvania. Hopefully, when this was all over, Etienne would abandon his American properties. Jules was done with rednecks.

Jules raised his hands and inhaled deeply trying to keep his body calm. The stiffness in the men, the heavy scent of fear and sweat on Minette and the visual reminder of gun, gun, gun and gun did not exactly suppress his adrenaline. His breathing would keep the wolf assured that he had control of this delicate situation. Or so he hoped. Because honestly, he wanted that side of him very close in case something went wrong.

"I think we all want the same thing," Jules said.

Sweets stifled a laugh.

"Is that so?" he muttered.

Jules glared at him. None of the men registered any acknowledgment of his statement.

"There's an imbalance in the world right now," Jules continued. One that he didn't even understand and now he had to explain it to these rednecks.

"Yeah," the leader finally said. "Satan."

"It's a little more complex than that," Jules said. "Can we put the guns away?"

All eyes turned to the leader. The small man lowered his rifle just enough that Jules was certain he could dash it and nab it, but the odds of the other three not shooting him were low. But it was enough of a sign to show Jules who the weak link would be.

"Nope," the leader said. "Not until we have the girl."

"She's Satan's prostitute!" the last man on the right yelled.

Minette rolled her eyes.

"First of all," she said, the tone of teen sass rolling out of her mouth without hesitation, "if I were Satan's prostitute, I would hope he'd take care of my tuition bills. Second, I haven't gotten laid in almost a year, Satan or no."

She huffed.

"Jesus," she said under her breath.

"You got a fancy car," the leader said.

"It's a rental," Jules said. "On the boss's credit card."

Now the leader tightened his eyes. His jaw clenched.

"Take off your shirts," he demanded, shoving the gun toward them.

All the men took another step in, tightening the semicircle around them. Bursts of silver light broke through the clouds. The storm had almost officially passed.

"Pardon me?" Jules asked.

"Take off your shirts," the leader repeated. "Satan's cohorts bear the mark of the beast."

Jules obeyed, pulling his soggy black turtleneck over his head. The leader tilted his head toward the smallest man of the group.

"Check," he said.

The man, a ginger, with just barely enough facial hair to make what might pass as a goatee, lowered his weapon and pulled a cell phone from his pocket. He turned on the flashlight.

These guys weren't completely backward, Jules thought.

The ginger approached, cautiously, a tiny step at a time. His body trembled and carried a nervous aroma. It pleased the wolf inside Jules. Focus, Jules told himself. From about a foot away, the ginger washed Jules' torso with the light. When he reached the back of Jules' shoulder, the young man froze.

"There it is," he reported.

Jules shook his head.

"That's a tattoo," he said. "The mark of the beast is a water droplet?"

"Tattoos don't sparkle," the ginger said uneasily.

Fils de putain, Jules thought. These idiots knew their stuff. What they knew and how they knew it didn't make sense, but they knew.

Sweets peeled off his sweatshirt, and unbuttoned his flannel He gave Jules the clearest look of 'What the hell, dude?' but his action was clear. He was in this with them. More manpower on his side. Finally, he pulled his t-shirt over his head. The ginger watched and canvassed Sweets' torso with his flashlight.

"He's clean," the ginger reported.

"The girl," the leader said.

The ginger now stood in front of them, in the middle, Sweets on one side, Jules on the other, a wide-eyed Minette between them.

"I am not—"

Jules interrupted her. "It's okay."

"I'm not taking off my shirt."

"Fine," Jules said. "You know what they want to see."

Minette sighed. She opened the cashmere cardigan from Chez d'Amille and stood before the rednecks in a sleeveless tank top. Jules reached over and pushed the shirt toward her bra strap, revealing the flame on her rear shoulder.

"Yup," the leader said. "You're all coming with us."

"We're not the devil's minions," Jules said quietly.

The ginger waved his gun at them as the others came toward them, corralling them in the direction they wanted everyone to travel.

"That's what the devil's minions would say," the ginger said.

"Come on," Jules said. "You're more of a minion to the devil than I am."

The ginger pulled back and thought for a minute. "Why?"

"You're a redhead."

"That don't make sense," he replied.

Jules deflated a bit, this was a historically ignorant crowd.

"Nice try," Minette said. "Can you... do the thing?"

"And get shot? No thanks," Jules said.

The men turned them and marched them toward an unseen destination. Sweets remained in the front, with the man who had yelled "Satan's prostitute" guarding him. Minette stayed in the middle, with the ginger, gun posed shakily. One swift snatch and Jules could disarm him. He had inherited the tobacco chewer at his side, and the leader played caboose. So he was the type of leader focused on mission and not his own ego. He did the important work.

Meanwhile, Jules concentrated on everyone's emotions. His sister seemed more angry than afraid, and Sweets' body language read stiffly, but his energy came off as distracted. And their captors were a mess. This scruffy crew would easily surrender their weapons, if the three shifters had a unified plan.

With the humidity out of the air, the cloud cover dissipating and the glow of the moonlight, the forest possessed a verdancy one couldn't detect in the daylight. The brown shades of decaying leaves and the thickness of tree trunks faded into the darkness, while to Jules' eyes, the hopeful greens of spring felt richer; the grass felt strong, the tiny plants erupting from the ground seemed powerful and lush, and every speck of a new bud on the branches overhead glittered.

But then he sensed a change in Sweets. Minette noticed it, too, because she suddenly stopped. The others almost stumbled into each other as the man paired with Sweets took several steps backward.

Sweets dropped to the ground, curling into himself, convulsing. Minette's eyes begged Jules for guidance. He had a split second to decide.

But it turned out the wolf inside him would make that decision even quicker. It was the swiftest, most intense change of Jules' werewolf experience, and the pain of his skeleton exploding into its animal form overtook him like an orgasm. There was no other way to describe the energy, the rush, and the certitude, the void of emotion, that came over him.

At the front of the pack, there stood a huge panther-esque cat with haunches as tall as Jules' own. The panther had already pounced on the man in the front, leaving the next in line to turn his rifle toward it. The unsteady man in front of Jules experienced such shock from the event that he couldn't move — yet. So, Jules turned to the ringleader. The leader had his rifle poised to shoot Jules right between the eyes.

The rifle pointed to the panther went off with a very loud, shaky sound. Jules leapt toward his own captor, jumping as straight upward as he could to avoid a bullet wound in the head. As he landed, his strong rear legs kicked away the gun, and he dropped the leader to the ground. One paw pressed the shooter's shoulder into the dirt, while Jules-as-wolf raised his other paw about to claw the man's face. Jules snarled and a viscous stream of drool extended from his muzzle almost to the man's nose.

And even in his animal state, Jules realized, he had never mauled a regular person. Self-defense or not, it struck something deep within him and he could feel his own humanity flux. And that quickly, he swiped his paw across the man's chest, enough to shred his shirt and leave deep scratches on his chest, the kind that left chest hair twisted into Jules's feet. And Jules, just as swiftly as the first transition, changed back to himself.

His victim screamed and writhed, more from confusion about what had happened versus pain or extent of injury. Jules walked to Minette, truly a beautiful creature in her animal form, and she licked the face of her captor, long and wet, as she stood on him, her back legs on his thighs and her front paws on his shoulders. He rocked his head back and forth, squinting and squirming and sputtering.

He turned to the panther. The panther similarly had detained his prey, but he sat on the groin of the final man, his gun beside him. Jules carefully crept toward it. The panther made cat noises akin to a purr but not as friendly.

Jules reached for the rifle.

"I don't think so," the ringleader said.

He had risen to his feet and had his gun honed on Jules.

"Let my man go," he demanded.

Sweets the Panther released him. The man grabbed his gun and scrambled to his feet. Jules surveyed the scene. They had ruined their clothes. Sure, the socks were fine but underwear and shreds of denim scattered across the woods like crepe paper off a beaten piñata. Minette transformed into her everyday self, as did Sweets. The three of them stood naked before their foes.

The three men who had been knocked to the ground— this all took place in probably less than five minutes— each slapped the ginger on the back of the head.

"This is your fault," the leader said.

Minette scurried around the torn clothes. She tossed on her cardigan and rummaged through the scraps but found nothing else remotely salvageable. Sweets grabbed one of the discarded guns. Jules picked up a few scraps of fabric that resembled clothes, handing others to Sweets and Minette.

The men tightened their circle around the three shifters, everyone now dressed in the shirts they had removed for their inspection and shredded pants. Sweets gazed to the cloud-covered moon.

"So, what are we going to do with you, mother of the anti-Christ?" the leader asked.

"Do I look like the mother of the anti-Christ? I'm not even pregnant," Minette replied.

"Gentlemen," Jules said. "You have this so wrong."

CHAPTER TWENTY THREE

The men brought the shifters to a trailer parked deep in the forest. It smelled of mold and contained more metal in beer cans that in the actual walls. The men sat the three of them on a musty orange-and-brown plaid couch as they paced the living room.

"We did it," the ginger said. "We found her."

"But what do we do now?" one of the other men said.

"We tie them up," the leader said. "And then we'll ask preacher."

That did not ease Jules' fears. There's a preacher? One of the men retrieved rope from a cabinet beside the refrigerator. The leader shook his head.

"They're animals," he said. "We hadn't anticipated that."

Ginger smiled. He disappeared into the hall. He returned with a length of chain.

"Silver," he said proudly.

"Dumbass, that ain't silver," the leader retorted. "But it is better than rope."

And that's how Jules, Minette and Sweets ended up bound to each other watching *Dukes of Hazzard* reruns guarded by rednecks drinking light beer from cans. Jules sat between Sweets and his sister. None of them could quite believe what they were seeing— Jules and Minette had never seen the show because of their upbringing in France and if Sweets had seen it, he didn't remember. Several episodes later, the trailer door opened. The preacher, a tall man in dark clothes and a cowboy hat, entered the living room. He sat down on the coffee table in front of them, so close Jules could touch him with his knees.

"What creatures of evil do we have here?" the preacher asked.

"Actually," Jules said. "We're the good guys."

"Is that so?" the preacher replied. "Werewolves are the devil's hounds, my son."

"I'm not a wolf," Sweets muttered.

"True," the preacher agreed. "Our prophecies did not mention you."

"So you know they're wrong," Jules said.

The preacher turned to Jules with a pointed, cold glare, even stronger than anything his mother would dish out.

"Boy," he said. "You have all the answers for someone chained up in the woods."

"What are you looking for?" Minette asked. Somehow, her voice sounded kind and empathetic.

"We're good Christian folk," the preacher said.

Jules huffed. "Because good Christians endorse kidnap—"

"Jules!" Minette interrupted. She looked directly at the preacher. "It makes sense, if you see supernatural creatures prowling the woods to kill them, right? But you didn't kill us."

"They might have," Jules snapped.

"I'm trying to understand the situation, Jules. Shut up."

The preacher smiled. "The prophecy said there'd be two, a brother and a sister."

"I'm new to this," Minette admitted. "And I'm not supposed to be a wolf. Is there any way that's a good thing? Like maybe God needed me?"

The preacher raised his eyebrows and scoffed.

"Babies themselves are inherently good," the preacher said. "But the baby we're looking for has the potential to destroy the world."

"Don't they all," Jules quipped.

"If raised right," the preacher continued, "that child could fix things."

"So, it's not the anti-christ?" Minette asked.

"We want the child."

"There's no child to give you," Jules said. "And who are you people?"

"We have our own community here," the preacher said, "where we gather and live according to God's principles while we wait for his corrective hand upon the world."

"Oh, Jesus..." Jules caught himself. "Forgive me. You're a doomsday cult."

The preacher shrugged. "We consider ourselves a Christian family. We don't care about the heathens outside."

"But we have no child," he repeated.

"If that's true," the preacher said. "She'll bleed. Or we could kill you all now to make sure."

"Maybe you're too late," Jules said. "Maybe the baby is already out there."

"Or you have the wrong mom," Minette insisted. "I mean, seriously. Do you really expect me to sit here chained up until I get my period?"

The preacher stood up, directed a gaze to his followers in the room, and looked back to them.

"For now," he answered.

The preacher walked out the door. Their captors relaxed as soon as he walked out the door. One hitting the fridge for another beer, the other slumping into his armchair to watch more reruns, and the third disappeared into the back hall of the trailer. Jules leaned towards Minette's ear.

"They are looking for Kait," he whispered in French.

She turned to him and made that "you're an idiot" face where her eyes turn to slits and her nose shortens.

"Okay," he continued in French. "That was a stupid statement. But do you think they're right?"

"Any child," she replied super softly, "has the capacity to fix things or destroy them."

"But is it nature versus nurture or something stronger," Jules said.

"Do you really think Étienne's DNA could yield the anti-Christ?"

"But Kait—"

"But isn't that why that other lady is involved?" Minette asked. "The baby is human."

The man watching TV glared at them. Jules did not reply. The man rose from his chair, awkwardly holding the rifle, and beckoned to the guy in the kitchen, the one drinking beer and scrolling on his phone.

"Hey, Danny," he hollered. "Let's move the girl. They're chatting."

Danny shrugged. "I didn't hear nothing. If we divide 'em up, it will be harder to watch them."

"Think we could shoot 'em?" the first one asked. "We only need the girl."

"I don't think you should be making any decisions."

Jules agreed with that statement. He studied the clumsy twists and turns of the chain that bound them. Minette had the smallest hands. Sweets probably had the most strength. But really, their best way out meant transforming, but Minette was inexperienced and Sweets couldn't control his. Jules decided to take the chance.

He dug deep into his chest, thought about what they had been through. The bruises and aches from the earlier battle with Adelaide, the emotions of reconnecting with Marissa, the fear of being marched at gunpoint through the wet, dark forest.

Jules turned to his sister, not seeing the woman that she was but remembering the girl he used to protect. And in the final moments before unleashing his inner wolf, he thought of the heat, and the humidity, and the salty smell of arousal and the tactile sensations of Jacqueline's flesh in the back of that army truck in Djibouti.

The chain shattered as it fell to the floor. Sweets and Minette leapt to their feet. Jules sailed toward their jailor with the rifle. The man in the kitchen drinking beer, Danny, ran into the living room and met, rather abruptly, Sweets' fist. Jules knocked his target to the floor, the gun fell. Minette grabbed it and hoisted it to her shoulder.

The third man, the one who had disappeared earlier, pounded through the hall. When he reached the scene, he found Jules-the-Wolf with one of his comrades on the floor, Sweets' brawling with the other and Minette aiming a shotgun at his face. He raised his hands in the air. Jules pressed one large wolf paw into his prey's throat. The man's legs swayed with desperation beneath him. Jules lowered his snout to the man's nose and snarled. The man froze. Suddenly, Danny tumbled to the floor.

"Shit," Sweets said. "I knocked him out."

Minette swung the gun around and smacked her target in the side of the head with it. He recoiled from the blow, and she whacked him again. He stumbled, and Sweets jumped across the room to grab his arms and force him to the floor. Minette grabbed the now broken chain. She and Sweets bound the two captives together, leaving only the man Jules had under him.

Sweets rooted through the kitchen cabinets and found rope and some zip ties. He and Minette restrained the final man in the bathroom. They had gagged the two conscious men before running out the door.

Jules used his werewolf nose to guide them to the car, which luckily Minette had the keys. He transformed back into human form and dressed from the clothes in the trunk of the Rolls. Minette grabbed a fresh outfit and changed in the car. Jules offered Sweets a pair of Lafayette sweatpants, which he accepted. The duo invited Sweets onto their journey, but he declined. He had more to find out about himself, but he might move his shelter under the circumstances. He promised he'd stay in touch.

CHAPTER TWENTY FOUR

They must have driven for an hour digesting what had just happened to them. Minette would mutter a "Can you believe?" and Jules would answer, "Yeah…"

If he had been with friends instead of a sibling, Jules might have tried to break the silence. But he knew his father's dictum, logic before emotion, caused them both to pause and reflect before reacting. He supposed, now, in hindsight, that Dr. Zweigenbaum had wanted to train his children, not out of some desire for properly masculine sons and a powerful, feminist daughter, but as a safeguard against his offspring transforming into monsters.

Literally.

So, really— he and Minette had no choice but to analyze the situation from as many angles as they could think of before speaking about it, determining their own theories and feelings before being influenced by the other.

Jules loved and respected his father— really, he did— but sometimes he wanted to act on the impulsive urge to punch a wall.

Minette finally committed to a conversation.

"So many things," she opened. "1. There are shifters other than werewolves. 2. He shifted in response to the full moon. That's just crazy. It makes no sense."

"The oceans respond to the moon. Tides change," Jules answered. "I've heard people say women's cycles often sync with the moon. And people, in general, do respond to the phase of the moon. Ask any ER doc."

"Or your Jacqueline."

"She's not my Jacqueline."

"You told her," Minette said. "And you talk about her all the time—"

"I needed help," he said, "and she had already figured most of it out."

"She saw you fumbling for Dad's pills and said, 'that guy's a werewolf.'"

"Min, just shut up."

More silence in the car. Even the radio played only static. Minette fiddled with it, and landed on a country station with the latest song from Blake Shelton.

"And the amnesia," Jules added. "The redneck doomsday cult. And the military? If we believe him on that."

"Why would he invent that?" Minette asked. "They might be looking for the doomsday cult. And we know that's real."

"Or they both know something is happening in that area," Jules replied, "like in Benji's TV show."

"The Hellmouth? Pennsylvania would be a way better place for it than California."

Jules chuckled. They drove for a while. Jules considered it recouping his strength from the strange night they had had. Minette thrust her shoulder between the seats in the front and stretched into the rear of the cabin. She reached for the champagne cooler that Benji had affectionately referred to as his snack stash, tugging it open and bumping Jules.

"Min, I'm driving," he snapped. "Stop hitting me."

She snaked into the passenger seat holding two half-pints of chocolate milk, which seemed a godsend right now. She popped open the cartoon with the expertise of a child in elementary school and handed it to him. He chugged it, flinching at the cold but watery chocolate juice that slid down his throat. He raised the carton into his field of vision: "no fat chocolate flavored milk."

"This shit is nasty," he told his sister.

She held her carton away from her with a grimace on her face. "Indeed."

And they shared a small, exhausted laugh.

"But I'm starving," Minette said.

Jules nodded. "The wolf thing takes a lot of energy."

Minette gazed at him. "Jules..."

"Yes, Min?"

He didn't want to take his eyes off Route 80 but something told him to look at her.

"Is this hard for you?" she asked. "Having someone else be a wolf?"

"Only because it's someone I love," he said, trying to disguise the feelings slipping into his voice. "Because on the other hand, it's nice not to be alone."

This time she nodded. And crumpling her milk carton, she sighed. "Blame Mom and Dad."

"Well, kids," Jules began, imitating their father. "When your mother and I met, there was no genetic testing like there is now."

Minette smiled. "But what did they think would happen?"

"I think they really thought, except for great-grandpa, there was no evidence that werewolves were real."

"Except for Grandpa William," Minette repeated.

"And I don't think they believed the stories about him," Jules said. "Could they have thought it was schizophrenic delusions? Psychotic break? Epilepsy and mental illness?"

"Spoken like the child of medical researchers," Minette quipped.

"Min, do you think they believed before I turned?" Jules asked. "Do you think they thought I was crazy? What was that like for them?"

"No," Minette said with rich certainty in her voice. "They knew. They just expected it to be Benji. I'd go so far as to say… Dad wanted a werewolf in the family. He's like the Victor Frankenstein of the modern age."

Jules felt his face scrunch.

"You know that Dr. Frankenstein stitched dead people, right?"

Minette sighed again.

"Jules, work with me here," Minette replied.

"But we're his children," Jules replied. "Who would want this for their children?"

Minette half-shrugged. "I'm the youngest, remember? The girl? Dad had more than the usual disappointment in my apparent biological sex and considering he had two sons, it didn't make sense. I think it was Mom that didn't take it all too seriously. She just supported her husband. But to Dad, I think proving werewolves are real means everything. Everything. Once he would sedate you…"

Minette explained how Dr. Benedict Zweigenbaum would hum excitedly, but nervously, as he cleaned up the aftermath of Jules' transitions. He would carry a tranquilizer gun around the house with this sharp glint in his eye that made Minette uncomfortable as a preteen girl. He would pace outside Jules' door, check his vital signs, and draw blood with a strange smile. And then he'd run off to his home office where she could hear the frantic clicking of computer keys.

"And that's why I won't tell him what's happened to me," she said.

It was Jules' turn to sigh.

"As much as I hate to stop the car so soon," Jules said. "I think we need to find a diner."

"And maybe someplace to take a nap?" Minette asked.

"We're less than three hours from your dorm."

"We really should rest. We haven't slept in almost a day. And maybe we should make some sort of record of what happened, and remember Étienne? Shouldn't we be looking for Étienne?"

They did have to figure out how they would track Adelaide, Kait, and Étienne. Until now, Jules had figured confirming that Adelaide was involved would be enough, that the guardians would finish it. But it was if he had conveniently forgotten that the guardians were in disarray.

He exited the highway in DuBois and pulled into the first hotel he saw— a Comfort Suites. They ended up in a room with a king-sized bed, and Minette quickly found the heavy plastic binder that contained pamphlets on what the town had to offer.

"There's a restaurant in an old train car!" she exclaimed.

She dropped to the bed, laid on her stomach, and spread the contents of the binder on the quilt, as she flipped through them.

"Goodie," Jules said flatly. As a chef, he hated gimmicks. "Is there a 24-hour diner?"

"This place is barely a town," she said. "It says here one of the attractions is the JC Penney at the mall."

She painted on extra exuberance and added, "Can we go?"

"That is so tempting," Jules said snidely as he sat on the edge of the bed, removing his shoes.

"We could go camping," she said, still paging through leaflets on the hotel desk.

"I've seen enough of the woods," Jules answered. "I'm exhausted, Min. Just find food. Room service?"

"The restaurant closed an hour ago," she said.

The siblings made eye contact. Minette nodded.

"Dominos or Papa Johns?"

"Depends what you can find," Jules said. "I don't want to end up at another convenience store."

"Green peppers and pineapple?" she asked.

"Yeah," he said, a sudden lightness in his heart.

When they were at home, he and Minette would always share a pineapple and pepper pizza and watch movies. Minette knew the drill. She called Domino's from the hotel phone. He grabbed some clean clothes from his suitcase and took a shower, inventorying bruises and scrapes from his recent incidents. Once dry, he slapped on some clean clothes and Minette dashed into the bathroom after him. She had a game of solitaire half-finished on the bed. He didn't know where she had found cards, but he enjoyed the distraction as he won her game.

The pizza arrived without issue, with an order of Parmesan bread bites. Jules scoffed with haughty disapproval when he saw the smelly dough balls laden with grease but, as the two of them demolished the pizza he was grateful for the extra food, even if it was mostly flavored oil and bread. Having two werewolves to feed made life more complicated. She sat at the head of the bed with the box of bread bites. He wished they had another pizza.

"We need to call Dad," Jules blurted out.

Jules sprawled across the end of the bed, hands folded behind his head and the empty pizza box open at his side.

"No," Minette said sharply.

"We've learned way too much in the last few days. We can't keep it to ourselves."

"No," she repeated.

"There are more types of shapeshifters out there," Jules said. "And you're not supposed to be a wolf, but you are. And what if Sweets is right? What if this is hurting you?"

He sat up. He sat cross-legged opposite her.

"No," she said a third time, but her resolve was weakening. He could hear it in her tone.

"Dad's on the other side of the country," Jules said. "We can keep the upper hand."

Minette sighed. "The rednecks in the woods claiming I was carrying the anti-Christ might have convinced me that Dad might not be unreasonable."

"This isn't about you," Jules said. "You're a byproduct. This isn't a human-caused dilemma."

"But didn't Étienne and—"

Jules raised his fingers to her lips abruptly. "I was there. You don't need to remind me. Yeah, they could have made a baby. But remember Kait's not the only mother. There's Sélène. So, the preacher is wrong. I mean, he has to be. Or we're on the wrong side. And I'm fairly certain we're the good guys."

"He said he wanted to make sure the baby was raised by the right people, the preacher," Minette said. "If we're looking at two moms, which one is right?"

Jules shook his head. "I don't think either of them would raise the anti-Christ."

"But if you had to choose?"

"Kait," Jules admitted. "But what about Étienne?"

"We don't even know where he is."

"Yeah but we're comparing mothers," he said. "Logically, Sélène would raise a child that would be normal, not even aware of this craziness. Kait would indoctrinate a child. But Étienne... maybe he's the middle ground."

"I still don't understand why I'm involved," she almost-shouted.

"Yeah," Jules agreed. "Did something... create a female werewolf? Or did the universe send me a companion fighter, but why not Benji? Why you? Why now?"

Minette gazed to the phone. "What time is it in California? God, like three o'clock in the morning?"

"No, you've got it backwards," Jules said. "Almost ten. At night."

He unhooked his cell phone from the charger on bedside table. He poised his fingers to dial.

"Go ahead," she said.

CHAPTER TWENTY FIVE

Jules tried to imagine the scene from his parents' perspective. Bedtime. A typical weeknight. Your son calls. At first, you're happy, knowing he could be in Paris or on the East Coast so the fact that it's late doesn't bother you.

At first, Jules didn't know what to say.

"*Coucou, maman*," Jules greeted his mother.

The small talk ensued. But Jules knew he had a mission. And Minette sat on his left side with her ear as close to the phone as she could get it without butting heads with him.

"*Maman*, we have something we have to tell you," Jules said.

"*Benoit*," *Maman* called to his father.

Jules turned to his sister. "Did you want to tell them?"

Minette shook her head violently.

"I hope Benji had a good flight," Jules said.

"Did he fly home?" Mama asked.

Typical Benji, Jules thought. He hadn't even checked in with their parents. Come to think of it, Benji didn't even text them to let them know he had arrived safely.

"I hope you all had a lovely time together," Mama said.

"Well, Mama, I'm glad you mentioned Benji's visit, because we needed his help because... Well... We've discovered that Min is a werewolf."

Their father grumbled something in the background that Jules couldn't distinguish because *Maman* cried out and wept. Minette rolled her eyes. Their father must have taken the phone because the whimpers sounded farther away and his voice came through the line strongly.

"Jules," Dad said. "You know that's not possible. Why would you upset your mother so?"

Minette took the phone from Jules.

"You always said it wasn't possible but I've had it happen a handful of times now, Dad. I'm a wolf. And I'm a girl."

"Are you sure?" their father replied.

"I have a vagina. I menstruate. And I just spent the evening chasing—"

Jules hissed at her.

"... Jules around the forest. As a wolf," Minette finished.

Jules leaned over the phone.

"I've seen it, Dad."

He grabbed the phone. "Do you remember the recent analysis you did for Jacqueline Saint-Ebène?"

Jules told them how he had gone to Jacqueline when he first discovered Minette's condition. He asked her to analyze some blood for him to see if she could diagnose why Minette wasn't feeling well. (Their father didn't need to know exactly how much Jacqueline knew or where the relationship between Jules and the military doctor had really gone.)

"And did she find anything?" Dad asked.

"So far, just that Minette has high testosterone levels."

"A-ha!" their father exclaimed, sounding a bit like Gene Wilder as Dr. Frankenstein.

Minette stole the phone back.

"Daddy, does that mean something to you?'

"It makes sense," he replied. "That's all."

It fits his testosterone and adrenaline theory, Jules thought. He didn't tell him about Minette's break-up, because that fit into his teenaged, sexual angst hypothesis.

In the end, *Maman* demanded that she and his father fly to Pennsylvania as soon as they could secure the tickets. And Minette agreed to the visit only if Dad would promise not to use her as a lab rat.

"I promise," he said. "Nothing more invasive than some blood tests."

Their parents still didn't know about the other supernatural realities of the world. And that Jules had no desire to explain. Jules needed to find Étienne, and Kait, even if he had no desire to see Adelaide.

"Depending what happens," Jules told Minette once he hung up, "I can't guarantee I'll be around when they get here."

Minette nodded. "Let's get some sleep."

Late the following morning, dangerously close to check-out time as he had Minette were justifiably exhausted, Jules packed up the car, paid the hotel bill, and took his sister to the restaurant in the train car. The 'diner' was more a village of sorts, with various businesses housed in the station or in the actual train cars, Amtrak to Conrail. From a distance, it looked like someone had parked the cars in some sort of railroad junkyard, jutting to and fro across a fairly broad parcel of land. It had everything from fine dining to pizza, ice cream to mini golf. This might be hard to justify to Madame as a business expense.

But it did seem like the kind of place where Étienne might stop and explore. So she might not question it if he used the corporate card, and the accountant was probably used to seeing it.

This place would not appeal to the current Étienne, the one wearing sweatpants, the Étienne who resurrected a dead supermodel. This place would greatly entertain the everyday Étienne.

The ice cream came from Penn State's Berkey Creamery, which had Minette forgetting about the idea of breakfast. Jules headed toward the diner car, hoping for a decent cup of coffee. That was when he started to understand that the whole complex surrounded a mini-golf course laden with dinosaurs.

He pulled out the vintage-style, red-and-white vinyl chair and sat at the small table, gazing out the window of the train car, where he could see Minette already had an ice cream cone in one hand and a putter in the other.

Jules turned the paper place mat to its blank side. He pulled a generic hotel pen from his pocket. He let himself doodle as he reflected on what he had learned. Kait had resurrected Adelaide. He didn't know what Étienne had possibly thought they were doing, but Kait knew.

When Adelaide opened the portal, she could have delivered her group anywhere in the world, or, if she understood it, anywhere in the fabric of time. But what had happened now that she had thrown Étienne in, without someone supernatural to guide and protect him? Jules didn't quite understand the quantum mechanics and relativity of it all, so he hoped Adelaide didn't either. Because he needed an advantage. But with Kait also in the fabric of space and time somewhere, he didn't really have anyone to explain the physics to him.

Oh, wouldn't that be something if the air-headed supermodel who planned to retire and open a shop selling wine paired with her homemade, fancy chocolates suddenly mastered theoretical physics?

What did he understand about the portals? From his own experience traveling through them, they bridged moments in space and time. The guardians existed outside space and time, and they relied on the same energy that kept the universe going.

So what people perceived as supernatural or paranormal was reality in a more fluid state. Is that how he would describe it? And the guardians or anyone who could perform magick or metaphysical healing could control that fabric of the universe. So an expansive geographical location like this planet... Well, someone who could manipulate perceived reality could skip the travel and merely reach into the space-time continuum and connect point A to point B.

"Hey, there," a voice said.

He twitched, the werewolf version of a jump scare. Way too many things were sneaking up on him these days. He turned, and a waitress stood beside him. She looked like a waitress, warm-faced, silver-haired, eyes laughing but smile a tad tired. She had an engraved name tag that said, 'Patsy.'

"You don't seem like a coffee guy," she said.

"I have had so much coffee in the last few days."

She gazed to his doodles. The paper contained circles, letters and lines. They all pointed into a larger circle on one side of the paper. So much for brainstorming.

"You look like you could use a classic malted milkshake."

"A classic?" he repeated.

"As American as apple pie," she replied.

He'd fallen deep into Americana with this road trip: major cities, rednecks toting guns, major highways, Tastykakes, hot dogs, processed cheese sauce...

"Do you have apple pie?" Jules asked.

"In a place like this?" she answered. "I think it'd be a crime if we didn't have apple pie."

"I'll take that malt," he said, "and how about a fried egg sandwich with..."

He smiled, but was cringing on the inside. "American cheese?"

The waitress nodded. "Sausage? Bacon? Pork roll?"

"No meat, thanks."

"And apple pie?" she asked.

"Yeah," he said. "I'd like some apple pie."

He really didn't, but he felt obligated. Patsy departed. Outside the window, Minette moved through the miniature golf course. Jules sighed and put down his pen, watching Minette chase the fluorescent green ball across prickly, outdoor carpet.

Where would Adelaide go? Her first instinct was to hang out at her grave, so what else would she think would strengthen her power? If she took the native soil thing seriously, would she pursue other elements? Or would she stick to places that had personal significance, like New York and Paris?

The waitress delivered his food. Few meals took less time to prepare than an egg sandwich and a milkshake. He finished the sandwich first, sipping occasionally on the malt.

So much had changed in so little time. And maybe the next step was to decide what he needed to do— and what he couldn't fix, a lesson Étienne did not understand.

Madame d'Amille obviously wanted her husband... ex-husband?... partner?... safe at home. Jules wanted his sister safe. Kait wanted a chance to keep her baby, which wasn't her baby, and who might be the anti-Christ if raised wrong.

What did Adelaide want? What would a dead person want if given another chance? Or... was the question really what would the magick do to her?

Minette popped into the diner car and dropped into the chair opposite him. Patsy hurried over to take Minette's order. Without hesitation, Minette asked for a tuna melt, French fries and a fountain vanilla Coke float.

"More ice cream?" Jules asked.

"How often do you get the chance to have a float from a fountain?"

"But you just had a cone," Jules continued.

"It's a full service fountain, Jules. They mix the syrup into the soda and then they add the ice cream," Minette said excitedly.

"I think I understand the mechanics," Jules said.

He lifted the bottle of Heinz beside the rectangular napkin dispenser.

"I also know how to make ketchup," he said.

She leaned on the formica table with both her elbows, her hands clasped and her face over his placemat.

"Do you know the difference between cat-sup and ketch-up?" she asked.

"No," he responded dryly.

She grunted. She looked down. Her glance moved around his empty plate to the drawing he had made. She pushed the plate aside.

"What's that?" she asked.

"Trying to sort my thoughts," he said.

She pulled the place mat to her and spun it on the table, studying it from various angles. She folded it up and put it in her pocket. Her sandwich and soda arrived. Patsy brought Jules his apple pie. Jules picked lazily on her fries. She glared at him.

"We can order more," he replied, "but you're on your second serving of ice cream so I think you won't starve."

She gave a one-shouldered shrug. A few seconds later, her fork was in his pie.

"Hey!" Jules exclaimed.

"We can order more," Minette retorted. "Oh, that's good."

She went for seconds.

"It is," Jules agreed.

They didn't use canned filling. He rarely found a diner that didn't use canned filling. He liked the natural crispness of the apples.

"And this is good ice cream. Apparently, Penn State has an ice cream-making program," she said. "Why am I studying engineering when I can have a bachelor's in ice cream?"

"Dad would love that," he answered. "Remember what happened when I enrolled in culinary school?"

"No," she replied, with a smirk. "I'm still scarred by the battle when Benji announced he wasn't going to college."

Jules nodded.

"Speaking of college, we're heading straight back to Easton," he said. "No more stops."

"No more werewolf games in the woods," she said.

"This whole thing makes me realize how much I don't know," he replied.

"Are you scared?" she asked between bites.

He pondered that.

"No," he said, "just confused."

Minette finished eating. She ordered a blueberry muffin to go. Jules almost asked for the rest of the pie. They paid the check, tipped Patsy handsomely, and returned to the Rolls.

CHAPTER TWENTY SIX

About three-and-a-half hours later, Jules dropped Minette off at her semi-suite in Watson Hall. When Jules left she was chattering to her roommate about her adventures in Paris and her new capsule wardrobe from her brother's boss. Their parents would arrive the next morning, so Jules planned to return the rental to Manhattan, see if Marissa had any free time to talk, and come back to Easton via commuter bus.

He brought the Rolls to the Chez d'Amille Manhattan office where the rental agency would retrieve it. John Clowes, Étienne's marketing director, ran to greet him. The six months that had passed since he saw everyone felt like a lifetime.

"Hey, John," Jules said.

In the last six months, it felt like everyone in the company had aged. John's dark hair seemed lackluster and his shoulders stood not-quite-so-straight, even his olive skin came across a little pale. The rumors had suggested that before all of this Madame d'Amille had wanted to close the New York office. That before Étienne's car accident and heart attack, before Adelaide's suicide that turned out to be a murder, before Alèxandre d'Amille's miraculous entry into the world, before all of it, while he was still a sous-chef in Paris, Étienne and Basilie had planned to condense operations, retire and raise a family.

"Good to see you, Jules," John replied.

Is it? Jules asked himself.

"While I'm here can I get you anything? Maybe we could gather everyone for some tea and cakes?" Jules suggested.

"You know it's 6 p.m.? I only stayed because I knew you were coming. Seema's the only other person here. And we didn't know if you had a key or the alarm code."

"I do not," he said. "So... Let me do what I have to do and get you all home."

Jules wandered to the kitchen out of instinct, and then corrected himself to head toward Adelaide's office. He didn't know if he was looking for a clue, or more insight. But he saw, thought, and smelled nothing.

Adelaide's office did not stand alone, it was part of Étienne's executive suite. Jules turned the corner and approached Seema's desk. She ruled the roost as his secretary. Étienne had a large private office behind her and Adelaide had a tiny office that connected to both Seema's reception area and Étienne's office. At one point the small room had been a closet.

"Hey, Seema," Jules said.

Seema smiled. She had a cheerful, earnest smile and always wore vibrant colors and patterns that complimented her dark skin. His phone buzzed with a text.

"It is great to see you, Jules," Seema said.

Jules read the message on his phone.

"Drink tonight after work?" Marissa asked.

Marissa wouldn't finish in the kitchen until at least eleven. If he stayed to meet her, he wouldn't be able to catch a Trans-Bridge bus until the following day. He'd need lodging, or he would have to sleep at Port Authority.

"Yeah," Jules said in response to Seema. "I wish I was here with less going on." She nodded.

"That face indicates you have a decision to make," she said.

"My ex wants to meet for a drink tonight," he said.

She smiled. "You still care about her."

"Very much," he said.

"Where do things stand now?"

"We reconnected when I was here last week."

"So what's the problem?"

"I didn't plan on staying in the city tonight. I don't have any place to stay," Jules said.

"I don't think you'll need a place to stay," Seema chuckled, "but if you do, you can turn up at the Peninsula at any hour. As long as you have the corporate card, they'll find you a place to sleep."

"But this isn't business," he protested.

"Do you know how much money Étienne spends at that hotel? Trust me."

Jules opened his phone. His thumbs hit the reply button.

"OK," he typed.

He texted his sister so she didn't wait up for him. He had planned on getting the last commuter bus from Port Authority at 9:30 p.m. He felt guilty for losing focus on his mission, but he wasn't sure what his mission was anymore.

Jules and Marissa met at the same Italian restaurant, but this time they sat at the bar. In a city of thousands of restaurants and thousands of bars, why did people prefer their regular spots? Familiarity? Ease? Habit?

Marissa had arrived first. She leaned with fatigue in her posture, even though the barstool had a chair instead of just a seat. She wore black trousers and a black tank top, her white jacket draped across her lap, her hair still contained with a bandana. For a brief moment, he missed the days of meeting her in similar attire with similar bone weariness. Tonight he was just tired because he was no longer accustomed to a bedtime of two or three a.m. He eased into place beside her, turning his chair toward her as he sat, with one arm on the bar and the other sweeping across her back.

"I'm happy to see you again," he said.

It sounded like a cheesy pick-up line. She turned, smiled, and pulled her hands away from the dark red beverage he assumed, based on experience, was a cosmopolitan. She gazed to the bartender, made pointed eye contact, and the man grabbed a glass and reached for a bottle. He placed a dark cocktail with a maraschino on the bar. Jules took it and sipped.

"Old-fashioned," he said. "The first time I had whiskey..."

His best friend had invited him to his grandmother's for dinner a few weeks before they moved from Biarritz to California. At that time, he couldn't even remember the name of the town in California. He was fourteen. Grandmother offered him an aperitif.

"Remember, this was still in France and my mother had allowed me to have a glass of wine with dinner since I was twelve," he told Marissa.

As if she could have forgotten his mother.

"Grandmother proudly showed me this bottle of American whiskey," Jules said.

So the first time he drank whiskey, he did a shot with his best friend's grandmother at Sunday dinner. Marissa smiled again. She'd probably heard the story before, but her eyes softened and told Jules that she didn't mind.

"What are you thinking?" he asked.

"You've changed," she said. "Grown, maybe? You're so confident now."

He shook his head and drank perhaps too much of the old-fashioned as it burned his throat.

"No, I'm still the same mess I always was," he replied. "Especially with you. I'm sweating here."

She made an uneasy but happy noise, a chirp maybe? A small laugh?

"You're an easy leader," she added. "The guy who leads the kitchen without thinking, without yelling."

They fell silent. How could he tell her that he was a terrified disaster? How could he expose her to the craziness of his world? Sure, she knew he was a werewolf, but did she really understand the depth of weirdness around him?

"Jules..." she said. "What happened between us then... and now..."

She turned to her drink for moral support. She fingered the lime wedge as if it were a baton.

"Would you come back to my place?" Marissa asked.

"Why?" Jules blurted out.

Marissa cocked her head and peered at him in disbelief.

"My *lièvre à la royale* lacks a certain *je ne sais quoi*," she replied.

Her playfulness made his heart jump. He set the cocktail on the bar, intentionally stared deep into her eyes, stroked her cheek gently as his other hand pulled her face closer. Her eyes closed in anticipation. His heart throbbed, as did something else.

He leaned in and kissed her, the kind of kiss that starts timid and slowly builds, the kind of kiss that both their bodies fell into, wanting to draw closer, the kind of kiss that reached deep inside and tethered to their souls. Their prior meeting had quenched the erotic desires between them— but it hadn't addressed the unspoken trauma of their past, the wound of how she ended their relationship, breaking a commitment Jules had made for a lifetime. Not that he blamed her. The whole experience at Notre Dame was shocking for both of them.

He pulled away. Her skin had flushed. He loved her vivid, red cheeks. He loved the softness of her mouth as she made facial expressions. He loved the way her cheekbones reappeared as they reached for her ears. He loved the smell of her building arousal as she stared in anticipation at him. He loved all of her. And he always would.

"Seeing you again..." Jules said.

He returned to his cocktail.

"I need to tell you everything," he said. "I won't ever keep a secret from you again."

The alcohol burned the lingering feminine scents from his nostrils. The sexual chemistry between them blinded him and he welcomed its erasure, even if brief. She nodded.

"Part of me died when you left," he said. "The joy. The hope. The part of me that believed I could live a normal life."

Jules put his cocktail back on the bar. He turned to her.

"I can't," he said. "I cannot get involved with you again and risk feeling that again. It would kill me."

"Jules, I—"

"Let me finish," he said. "You are my mate. I know that now. And if you want me in your life, I'm here, one hundred percent. But you need to think about it, long and hard, because I'm not just a man, but I'm also a wolf, and now that my sister has turned, I have a pack to protect."

Marissa offered a nervous laugh.

"That sounded darkly stalker," she said quietly, "but I know who you are."

They nursed their drinks. Jules focused on the tart notes of the cranberry juice lingering in his mouth, which was the taste of her mouth, and the curve of her lips.

"I can't go home with you tonight," he said. "I want to, but you don't need physical responses coloring your decision."

She chuckled again. "As if I haven't thought about you every day."

The smell of her surrounded him— her sweat from her shift at the restaurant, the food odors from the kitchen (onions, garlic, definitely basil, and so much thyme), the gel she put in her hair so it wouldn't break free from the bandana. She even wore the same anti-perspirant that he remembered, lavender and coconut but not coconut like the fleshly interior but the heaviness of the oil. And maybe if he concentrated, he could sense the chemical aroma of her mascara, the only makeup she wore to work.

And why would he want to identify such a scent?

Anything to prevent dwelling on the sweet, tangy shift in her hormones and the desire emanating from her pores... and other more intimate places. After their tryst last week, the scent revived flavors and feelings and physical memories. The encounter with her had reminded her what it felt like to love and merge with a woman. The raw meeting with Jacqueline prior had released something primal. Jacqueline, as unpredictable and impulsive as she was, had taught him more about how much of his nature he could control, something his father had insisted was impossible without pharmacological intervention.

And did Jules really just tell Marissa that he had a pack to protect?

"Jules," she said softly. "You drifted away somewhere."

He nodded. "I'm really happy to have this second chance with you."

She smiled and reached for his hand.

"Me, too. If I'm going to walk this path with you..."

Nervousness washed over her, rising from her flesh like humidity evaporating from asphalt on a brutal summer day. He sensed what she wanted to ask, even before the words left her lips. He shuddered.

"Can I meet the wolf?" she asked, in a tone not more than a whisper.

"That's fair," he replied.

He hoped she could not sense the shift in his mood, his discomfort, the way his heart clogged his throat as terror consumed him.

"But that's what scared you away last time," he said.

She shook her head.

"No," Marissa said. "It was shock. And confusion. And the whole situation."

She finished her drink and ordered another. She held a finger up to the bartender, gazed at Jules, and smiled.

"Can you mix me two shots of half Sambuca and half Chambord?" she requested.

The bartender responded with a chin-led nod.

"The Good 'N Plenty," Jules said. "I haven't thought of those—"

"Since those long winter nights?" she replied.

The bartender placed the shots on the bar, and Jules noticed a third on the inner rail. The bartender downed the extra.

"Nice," the bartender said as finished and walked away.

Jules and Marissa lifted their glasses and swallowed the contents in unison.

"We've both grown up a lot since that night," Marissa said. "Plus I live in the East Village now, so I don't scare as easily."

He laughed. It was quiet, but genuine. The licorice and raspberry flavors of the alcohol burned his throat and warmed his body. He reached for her, pressed his palm against her cheek, and she pressed into his hand. He leaned into her and kissed her tenderly. He motioned to the bartender for another round of shots.

CHAPTER TWENTY SEVEN

Jules willed his human consciousness not to fade. He peered at Marissa through the muted vision of the wolf. She came alive in ways he could not explain. Her scents, her sounds, and her presence layered in a way that a human could not perceive. Jules relaxed into the setting— Marissa's old, typical walk-up apartment. He released the hyper-vigilance of the predator and allowed himself to trust his surroundings.

Her movements as she reached for the side of his dark muzzle seemed clunky and predictable. Part of his brain reminded him that he could tear her arm off swiftly if he so desired, but his calm heart rate and lowered defenses meant he wouldn't. The intensity of the city outside the apartment distracted him— the traffic, the throng of people, the flickering lights, the urine, the beer, the sweat, the arousal, the vermin, the rotting food, the lingering scent of blood, and the endless human chatter— an endless blend of dirt and human construction with the scrappiest of nature fighting to survive.

Her hand landed beneath his ear. She scratched. She buried her hand in his soft undercoat. No one had ever touched him in wolf-form. He tilted into it, ever so slightly, not totally releasing his guard.

"You're beautiful," she said in an awe-struck, breathy tone that told him she really meant it. "You're like a giant Siberian husky."

He cocked his head and gave her a tiny growl. Did she really just compare him to a dog? She removed her hand. She trembled, barely perceptible. His growl had startled her. In this form, he couldn't tell her it was all right. He couldn't talk to her. So, he dropped his front paws and laid down. He set his head on his legs. He looked up to her. She smiled. She stroked the back of his head and continued petting his withers.

A struggle erupted in his wolf brain. He should not allow the human to touch him, the inferior species, the prey. But then he looked at her, all soft and squishy and full of gentle emotions. He laid across her full bed, which was barely big enough to accommodate his height as a human let alone his massive self as a wolf. She lowered herself beside him, sitting on her knees. He swept his head to the side and laid it on her lap. She giggled, a nervous response at first, but then her posture relaxed.

No one had ever touched him before.

He carefully rolled away from her, exposing his thick belly hair. She looked at him, her view askance with distrust.

Do I look like a cat? he thought.

She reached down and buried her hand in the fur there. She moved in her jerky, human way and did something completely unexpected: she snuggled into him, spooning inside his wolf body. He instinctively flicked his tongue into the air tasting for any trace of her reproductive hormones.

Marissa curled tightly into him. Nothing about her body indicated fear or nervousness. And she leaned her head against one of his legs, using it as a pillow. And before he realized it, she was asleep. Her body had fallen into a still rhythm. Her breathing and heart slowed. And so, he slept, and he couldn't remember ever sleeping in wolf form before— and tranquilizer darts and pharmaceuticals did not count as sleep.

And then he woke, next to her, as a human. He rolled carefully onto his back, stared at the ceiling, and pondered. What had just happened? He extended his hands in front of his face in the darkness, moving them into the thin line of orange glow creeping into the apartment window. Human fingers. He had transformed without realizing it, without the pain and the struggle.

He gazed to Marissa, tucked in the fetal position, still in her clothes. He slid her hair away from her face and kissed her forehead. Then, he went back to sleep.

In the morning, after a simple breakfast of eggs Benedict, Jules left Marissa and bought a ticket for the commuter bus from Port Authority to downtown Easton. To kiss him goodbye, Marissa had stood on tip-toe. She pressed her body into his while resting her hands on his hips and almost managed to pull him into bed with a sweet dance of her mouth. He had almost succumbed to the instinct. Instead, he would treasure the memory of the kiss.

Her version of the wolf— of him— resembled a fairy tale, and like a fairy tale, she needed to think about which creatures could be trusted and which would lead her into an enchanted forest. He would not influence her decision by appealing to her physical desires.

Jules' parents' plane had landed in Newark, N.J., two hours earlier, so they might all converge on Minette at the same time. And ironically, depending what bus Jules took, they could all arrive on the same vehicle, but Jules knew his parents would rent a car.

And that was fine, because Jules still had a supernatural mission— to find the sire— which he had done, technically, but he realized his responsibility to Kait extended further.

But how far? What could he do for her? Did the universe really expect him to protect her unborn child?

Buses lend themselves well to contemplation. So Jules used the two hour bus ride to think.

He also thought about Minette. Jacqueline had suggested that Adelaide set something in motion... And Sweets had suggested Minette's body couldn't handle life as a werewolf.

He had to make some plans, and it felt like there was no one left to help him decide on his actions.

The bus station in Easton was about a mile from Lafayette's campus. He didn't tell his family he had arrived. He walked through the downtown to the century-old stone steps that wove up the wooded hill where the founders had built the school. It was strangely isolated. He passed a statue, and it resembled someone from hundreds of years ago, staring to Easton below as a protector.

Jules emerged between stocky, brick buildings, probably dorms, and he continued walking across the quad toward Minette's dorm. He texted her once he reached the building. She appeared wearing one of the d'Amille dresses, which from what he had seen of the students, would fit in on this campus.

"Hey," she said.

"Are they here?" he asked.

"Yeah," she said. "I've been somewhat obscure about our trip."

"Let's keep it that way," he said.

She turned and headed toward her room. When they got there, the only other person in the room was Minette's roommate.

"Where's Dad and *Maman*?" Jules asked.

"They went to check into their room and freshen up," Minette said.

She flopped onto her bed, sitting, and opened a thick book from one of her engineering classes, judging from the text and graphs. Her roommate waved.

"Hey," the roommate said.

"Hey," Jules replied.

He carried Minette's desk chair past the open closet, where all the other d'Amille items now hung, and placed it near the end of her bed.

"No other problems?" Jules asked his sister.

"Problems?" Minette asked.

"Nothing suspicious?"

Jules didn't want to scare the roommate, especially since he didn't know what she might know about the break-in.

"No," Minette said. "But I keep an eye out for pick-up trucks."

"You think that's what happened?" he asked.

Minette shrugged. "They did seem to know where we were."

"So what's the plan?" he asked.

"With *Maman* and Dad?" she responded.

He nodded. "Do we tell them?"

Minette peered at her roommate, who despite her feigning indifference was listening to the conversation.

"They are at the Lafayette Inn," Minette said. "I don't know how much of our trip you'd like to share with them, but we are adults. They can't be that mad that we didn't tell them we took a road trip to Chicago."

"Okay," Jules said.

"Dad says he has some work project and there's some guy locally who can help."

"Oh, really?" Jules asked.

Minette shot him a glare.

"I told you Dad would make this a work trip," she said icily. "The parents want us to talk about it after dinner."

"I'll be here, Min."

"Anyway," she said, angrily turning the page in her book. "I have homework to do."

"Well, what should I do?" he asked.

"Go straight out this dorm, down High Street past the Williams Center, to Cattle Street, turn left and walk two blocks."

"Where will that take me?"

"To *Maman* and Dad," she replied.

"Then why didn't you tell me to go there in the first place?"

"Because I didn't know you'd be a dick."

"I'm not a dick. I just asked about our parents."

"I have—"

"Homework," Jules interrupted. "I know."

He stood, grabbed the chair much less delicately than last time and shoved it back to the desk.

"I'll show myself out," he muttered.

"I told you this would happen," she snapped.

He tossed his hands in the air. As he walked down the hall, his wolf ears heard her roommate.

"Margot," the young woman said, "You were really mean to your brother."

"Not your problem, Jamie," Minette replied. "And I don't use my given name."

"But Margot is so pretty," Jamie said.

Jules chuckled as he reached the door. A book slammed. Minette ran into the hallway, text and notebook in hand, with a pen sticking from the spiral.

"I'll come with you," she said. "Can we stop at Wawa?"

"You need something at the convenience store?"

"I guess we don't have to," she said.

"I could use a bottle of water," he said.

She smirked. "D'ac."

The tiny market overflowed with college students, most waiting for sandwiches. Jules grabbed a bottle of Perrier. Minette had a soft pretzel and a red, frozen beverage. She slapped her items on the cover and peered at him.

"Oh, I'm paying?" he remarked.

Her face dropped into a pout.

"I don't have a job, big brother," she said.

He sighed and placed his water beside her treats.

"Don't you have meal plan?" he asked.

"Yes," she said, dragging out the end of the word, "but you and I both know it will be eight o'clock by the time our parents take us to dinner."

"So, theoretically, you could have an early dinner on campus—"

"Yes, and leave you alone with Dad's questions. Because this is all your fault. I'm the baby. You're the middle child."

The cashier slid the items across the crowded counter. Jules retrieved his wallet.

"Do you need a bag?" the cashier asked.

"Nope," Minette answered, swiping her items.

"Thank you," Jules said as he put away his debit card.

He grabbed his water and uncapped it. When they walked outside, the mid-afternoon sun washed over the street, blending the majestic, golden glow with the drab exteriors of single-family homes tucked side by side that had been converted into businesses. A seafood purveyor, a selection of pizza places all grouped together like a pizza district, an abandoned gas station, and a chiropractor among them. Students flocked to the Wawa, the parade never-ending, like ants descending upon forgotten crumbs. Minette continued down the sidewalk, chomping on the pretzel and then slurping her red confection.

"Are you settling back into school?" he asked.

She pivoted, stared at him and raised her eyebrows. "Yeah. Since when do you ask about school?"

Jules shrugged. "You're the smart one, Min."

"Can you remind Dad of that when we get there? Because I still have a 4.0. And..." She paused. "Jules, you promise me... I don't want to be Daddy's little science experiment."

"How far is this place?"

She pointed diagonally. "End of the next block and it's right there."

"Unless he has the tranq darts ready, we can take him," Jules said.

Jules chuckled at his own joke.

Minette smiled. "That's not funny."

Her face paled. She opened her mouth. She exhaled.

"Min?"

They stood at the corner of High and Cattell Streets, only one house from the Wawa, in the shade.

"How is this so amusing to you?" she questioned.

"You have to laugh," he said, "or you're going to cry."

"I remember that night at the dining room table, when Dad pulled a gun on *Maman*." She paused, shredding the pretzel and shoving it in her mouth. "I thought he was going to shoot her. You morphed into your wolf shape and threatened him. Dad has said you were a wolf. But..."

Jules touched her shoulder.

"I watched your body break apart and then change into this beast," she continued. "I don't think he warned *Maman*. She was so red, and shaking, and we were all screaming. Benji, me, *Maman*. And then, he shot you! Except I didn't know it was tranq darts. He hit you twice and you fell on the table like bricks."

She had valid reason to fear their father. He never considered what it must have been like to witness that scene.

"I thought you were dead," she said. "I thought our father had killed you. So none of this is a joke, Jules."

CHAPTER TWENTY EIGHT

Growing up Jules had known that his father, Dr. Benedict Zweigenbaum, had penned some of the greatest studies in genetic disorders which led to the development of medications which changed the lives of people who had such conditions. Benedict often pined that he could not do more to fix sickle cell anemia and obsessed over obscure disorders like Prader-Willi Syndrome. As children, the Zweigenbaum siblings had no idea what fueled their father's curiosity. That changed when Jules made his first transformation.

And if you ever wanted to visit Bizarro World (without Superman), imagine your father gathering the family at the dining room table to announce that you had inherited and activated the lycanthropy gene.

Now, Jules and Minette sat in dark leather armchairs, side by side, under small windows, with a charming stove in the corner. *Maman* sat on the bottom corner of the king-sized bed, poised upon the plain but chicly-patterned white comforter, her hands crisply folded in her lap. Her dark hair and perfect posture seemed appropriate in front of the batik wallpaper. The art featured what appeared to be a man and a woman in nineteenth century in the woods, which, because it was wallpaper, rolled down the wall in a deep, red pattern that matched the pillows.

Dr. Zweigenbaum wore khakis with a crisp seam down the front. Unlike Étienne who ironed everything he wore (a habit the man never abandoned even as he gained wealth and stature), Jules' father had his laundry sent out. *Maman* would rather have a glass of wine and assemble a delightful, artery-clogging cheese platter that smelled like old shoes than iron Dr. Zweigenbaum's pants in this outdated manner. Dr. Zweigenbaum wore brown loafers and a brown belt, with his not quite peach, not quite beige collared shirt with a few creamy-colored lines creating a mild checked pattern.

"Dad," Jules said. "Did you take that shirt from my closet? I'm pretty sure that was one of my bad choices in high school."

His father said nothing to acknowledge the comment and stood at the end of the bed, inches away from them, his two youngest children. And Jules could feel the vibe coming off of him— you idiots, I thought Benji was the one I couldn't trust— and Jules didn't need his werewolf senses to interpret it. Minette winced under the pressure. As the baby, the girl, the smart one, she had never come under the kind of scrutiny and disappointment they faced now. Jules turned toward her, offering her a faint smile.

"Look at me, Jules," his father said. "I can't believe you two are in cahoots."

Cahoots? Jules had to stifle his snicker.

"This isn't funny," his father said.

Jules had failed at hiding his reaction.

"Dad—"

"I'm not ready to hear anything else from you," Dr. Zweigenbaum interrupted. "How could you not tell me?"

Jules didn't answer, because Dad clearly wasn't ready for Jules to speak.

"Well?" his father asked.

Somehow, everything connected to Jules. Was this the plight of every middle child? You were supposed to learn lessons from your older brother, protect your younger sister, keep the peace, stay out of the way...

"I'm waiting," his father said.

And frankly, Jules thought, I'm twenty-six. I'm too old for this shit.

"Dad," Jules finally replied. "Min has worked really hard and she's grappling with this. We both are. You told her she wouldn't inherit the condition. And she did. So she came to me."

"You should have come to me," Dr. Zweigenbaum said to her.

"I was what... ten?... when Jules changed? You had just moved us from France... and that was a big adjustment," she explained. "And then I saw Jules beat the shit out of this kid, and it was really cool, and you and *Maman* came to school separately to bring us home."

"None of us expected that day," *Maman* muttered in French.

Jules thought he sensed her fighting the urge to cry. He rose, and against his father's angry looks, he went to his mother, sat beside her on the bed, and touched her knee.

"Please don't worry, Mother," he whispered to her in French. "I will always watch out for Minette."

"I know," she said and patted his hand. "Part of me wishes we had never had children, but I look at your faces and I love you so much."

"You trusted a French military doctor with your sister and your sister's medical data," their father said.

Jules nodded. His father had analyzed the samples from the fetuses of Madame d'Amille and Sélène, the human mother of Kait's baby. The tests suggested the babies shared Étienne's DNA, despite the fact that Étienne had seen Sélène since 1978. His dad didn't know all that. His dad merely did the DNA tests.

"We were in France, and she has been extremely helpful," Jules said. "She has a fresh. and detached, outlook on this whole thing."

"She knows?" Dr. Zweigenbaum said. "She knows knows?"

Jules shrugged at first, but as his face fell with the gravity of his mistake, he changed the gesture to a nod.

"Yeah, Dad. I told her."

"Why would you tell a French military doctor that you're a werewolf?"

"She was figuring it out, Dad. Not the werewolf thing, but she'd seen me have 'seizures' and found me naked in the desert. She read my pill bottle and wondered why you had me on enough psych meds to tranquilize an angry bull. So, I mean, what choice did I have?"

"I told you. You have a rare seizure disorder—"

"Dad, she watched my jaw dislocate."

Dr. Zweigenbaum exhaled so hard that his lips vibrated.

"Look," Jules said. "I know this isn't the way you would have done things, but it's the way it's happened. She's known for more than a month. Nothing has happened. And if you're interested, she gave us an fMRI."

His father's frustrated demeanor faded.

"And we're not in a military prison," Jules added. "Which, should that ever happen, you can alert the American embassy. I don't think either country will want the children of a prestigious medical researcher embroiled in some sort of incident."

The hostility in his father's mannerisms transformed as Jules retrieved a compact disc from the backpack of possessions he'd been carrying all day. Dr. Zweigenbaum accepted the disc from Jules and moved toward an invisible desk, eager for a computer to load the reports inside.

"I was scared, Daddy," Minette said, using the child-like voice she always saved for their father. "You said I couldn't be a werewolf and I am. And I know you don't mean it, but you would put that mystery first."

"Oh, honey, no..." Dr. Zweigenbaum said.

It was then that their mother rose and approached her husband.

"The children are right, Ben."

"A female hereditary werewolf?" Dr. Zweigenbaum said.

"Dad," Jules said. "Hereditary? So, there are other wolves?"

"I did not mean to imply that," Dr. Zweigenbaum said.

"That's not a denial, Dad."

"I don't know, Jules. My research has been rather confusing and inconclusive."

"In that case... A few days ago we met another shapeshifter," Jules revealed.

"Shapeshifter?" Dr. Zweigenbaum repeated. "There's no such thing as shapeshifters..."

"You can try to believe that, Dad," Jules said.

"A panther, Dad," Minette said with vigor in her voice. "He appeared to change with the full moon."

"That's ridiculous," Dr. Zweigenbaum said.

"Is it?" their mother asked. "You didn't really believe this was the only mutation out there? Just because our science can't explain it, well, that doesn't mean it doesn't exist."

Dr. Zweigenbaum lowered himself to the end of the bed. He surveyed his family, and Jules could feel the power, the weight of his thoughts. Jules got to witness a change in his father's worldview. That's something a lot of people wish for but rarely get to see.

"Dad," Jules said. "This is all really complicated. Maybe I should tell you everything..."

CHAPTER TWENTY NINE

"He took that well," Minette said with a chuckle as she and Jules returned to her dorm.

The night had grown cold, and on the top of the hill where the college existed, the wind carried a bite. Jules had purchased a six-pack at the bar in the middle of the block, which was now in a plain brown paper bag. Minette ushered him into her room, where she took the sack and put four of the beers in the mini-fridge.

"Don't get busted," he warned.

She had two long necks balanced in one hand like a pro.

"I'm half-French. You and I know I've been drinking most of my life."

Jules gave a slow nod, reaching for one of the bottles. She passed it to him.

"I think *Maman* used to give us all apricot brandy," he replied.

"She said it was good for us," Minette said.

"You remember?"

Minette nodded.

"Where's your roommate?" Jules asked.

Minette read the clock on her desk.

"There's a study group that meets tonight. A bunch of the engineering majors get together to work on the problems for class."

"Should you be there?" Jules asked.

"Probably," she said. "I'll catch up."

Jules scanned the room for a bottle opener. Minette picked up an old metal fork and used the tines to loosen the cap, then she tossed it to him. He caught it. She sat on her bed. He turned her desk chair to face her.

"You okay?" Jules asked.

"I guess," she said, following that with a long drink. "Every time I think things could feel more upside down..."

Jules laughed.

"What is happening, Jules? Why do we exist? Why do I exist?"

Jules shrugged.

"The last couple weeks have opened my eyes," she continued. "But I'm glad it happened this way. I'm glad I had you. I'm relieved we told Dad."

"Me, too."

Jules spun the bottle as he struggled to raise his eyes from his own knees. Lost in his thoughts, he stared vapidly. How could he tell his sister how tormented he felt? He hated the idea that she had to share this life with him, but he also knew he now had a companion who understood. He thought about everything he had lost— and gained, especially now with the prospect of Marissa being back in the picture.

And he had questions, questions that perhaps Minette hadn't thought of yet because of their difference in age. Did all of this change her trajectory?

"What's next?" he asked.

She wrinkled her face and tossed up her hands as if reminding him that he was an idiot.

"I'll finish the semester. Maybe go to some yoga classes. And there's a summer program that I heard about in geology class, studying volcanoes in the Aleutian Islands up in Alaska."

They drank silently for a few minutes.

"What about you?" she responded.

He offered her a forced and tired smile.

"I don't know," he said. "I don't know if I have a responsibility to go after Kait, or Étienne, or Adelaide. And there's still the question of the baby Kait is carrying. Is it good or evil? And Sélène. And what is happening with the Guardians? So I guess I keep looking."

Jules reached toward his sister, about to drop his empty beer bottle in the trash can. A pain seared through his shoulder. He missed the garbage bin. The bottle rolled across the floor. Jules' arm jerked and within the corner of his peripheral vision, Minette curled into herself and spilled her remaining beer on her comforter. The carbonation hissed as they both recoiled.

Jules reached his hand to the opposite shoulder and held it. Minette laid in the fetal position on the bed. Jules rose, tiptoed across the room, and peeled back the short sleeve of Minette's dress.

Her glittery flame tattoo was gone.

"Min," he said. "I think we've been fired."

ABOUT THE AUTHOR

The beauty of words has infiltrated the life of Angel Ackerman for her entire life — from reading *Green Eggs and Ham* thousands of times to writing groundbreaking poems titled "My mom wears flip-flops" in Mrs. Sanders' second-grade class. She started the *Fashion and Fiends* series at the age of 16 and rewrote the novel *Manipulations* at least ten times before declaring this version "the one" in 2016.

Angel spent 15 years as a print journalist, specializing in weekly newspapers where reporters learned to write about every topic and take their own photographs. With the decline of print media, Angel explored the non-profit sector where she worked in public relations, program design, social media, grant writing and development.

Although now separated, Angel enjoyed a 20-year marriage to poet Darrell Parry who proved pivotal to bringing Angel's fiction writing career to fruition. Angel and Darrell both have disabilities. Angel had mild cerebral palsy which she has embarked on a journey to understand more about. Darrell has a club hand. They have an able-bodied teen daughter, Eva, who keeps bringing home strays — leaving them with a current count of four cats, one pit bull/black lab/mastiff puppy, one goffin cockatoo, one parakeet and multiple foster cats from their volunteer work with Feline Urban Rescue and Rehab.

Angel holds a bachelor's degree in English Language and Literature and French from Moravian College, a bachelor's in International Affairs (with honors) from Lafayette College, and initiated a master's degree in World History at West Chester University. Her academic interests include French post-colonial

Africa, Muslim relations, and the politics of miscegenation. She hopes to revisit her honors thesis which looked at the stereotypes of Muslims in France and how they continue the thought process of the colonial era. The update would encourage readers to compare the attitudes of European Imperialism to modern race/minority relations.

In addition to Lehigh Valley, Pa., newspapers, Angel has been published in *Ten Word Stories* by *Dime Show Review, Rum Punch Press, StepAway Magazine,* two volumes of *The SAGE Encyclopedia,* and did book reviews for *Hippocampus Magazine* and *Journal of Global South Studies.* She currently writes for *Armchair Lehigh Valley* and *Kiss and Tell Magazine.*

When not examining the world with a post-colonial critical theorist's eye, Angel loves to travel and study foreign languages. She has visited Canada, France, Tunisia, Somalia, Djibouti, Yemen and various parts of Russia (such as trekking to Siberia for pizza). Read more of her escapades at AngelAckerman.com and follow her on YouTube, LinkedIn and Instagram.

AVAILABLE NOW!

Find the first three books in the Fashion and Fiends series at your independent bookseller or online at Barnes and Nobles and Amazon.com.

MANIPULATIONS Weirdness surrounds Adelaide Pitney, former house model at Parisian fashion house Chez d'Amille. It always has. When she meets Galen Sorbach, an aspiring photographer, she hopes she's found a normal boyfriend, for once.

She doesn't realize that Galen has been stalking her for latent healing powers, water magick she's used accidentally in large quantities. A fire mage, Galen never mastered water magick. Adelaide's gifts could be the power he needs to depose the Spirit Guardian and become a god.

Galen's sister, Kait, has spent 400 years as the elemental water guardian. Assigned to subdue Adelaide's magick, Kait delays. Her reluctance allows Galen to manipulate Adelaide and threatens the safety of the person Adelaide loves most, couturier Étienne d'Amille, and his lover, Basilie.

These five people — a 400-year-old Irish witch, her adopted psychopathic brother, an American supermodel, a French fashion designer, and his rich ex-wife — find their lives intertwined as they explore how far they will go for love and how much they can forgive.

COURTING APPARITIONS World famous fashion designer Étienne d'Amille knows he should be grateful. He's survived several personal tragedies and almost died. He and his ex-wife, Zélie, will welcome their first born child into the world after 20 years of infertility. But grief has crippled Étienne. And his depression has threatened his relationships. So many questions linger about recent events: Did he take advantage of his protégé/supermodel Adelaide Pitney? Did he miss warning signs that could have prevented everything? And when Étienne's just about to crack — he discovers his house is haunted and the ghost stuck there begs him to free it before familiar supernatural creatures kill them all. Did Étienne receive the second chance he wanted? Or will he plunge into a magickal universe he's not equipped to understand?

RECOVERY Dr. Jacqueline Saint-Ebène joined the French Defense Health Service because she had grown bored of vaginas. But neither her years as an Ob-Gyn nor her tour as a combat surgeon in Africa prepared her for her latest assignment: a supernatural immaculate conception, her pregnant oldest sister's stroke, and the army's concern that her brother-in-law might exist as the center of it all.

While Jacqueline grapples with family and military drama, she also finds herself in a personal crisis in Djibouti. She underestimated the role of Issa Somali culture in her boyfriend's life and learns he has a secret that threatens the core of their relationship.

Throw in a sexy young werewolf— and, yes, werewolves are real — and Jacqueline doesn't know where to find the truth.

Anticipated 2025!
The *Fashion and Fiends* Series Continues

ABSOLUTION Celebrated couturier Étienne d'Amille abandoned everything — the woman he loves, his long-wished-for, newborn baby and a successful fashion empire — to follow Kait, a 40-year-old Celtic witch, to Chicago where they resurrect his beloved, murdered muse, supermodel Adelaide Pitney.

Étienne quickly realizes nothing is what it appears. Adelaide throws the supernatural guardians of elemental power into anarchy, Kait is carrying a child conceived 25 years ago, and a doomsday cult thinks Étienne and his ensemble will birth the anti-Christ.

Étienne and Kait soon find themselves as hostages and Étienne must face emotional and physical torture before an unlikely hero, or maybe the most logical hero, calms the chaos and returns balance to the creative forces of the universe.

The question becomes: Will Étienne survive?

FINDING HOOYO After rescuing her brother-in-law Étienne d'Amille from a resurrected supermodel and a doomsday cult, combat surgeon Dr. Jacqueline Saint-Ebene makes the ultimate deal with the devil — she agrees to an American-led NATO mission in Afghanistan.

She quickly finds her niche in providing maternal and other female-centered care. When she loses most of her unit when the Taliban mounts an ambush of her clinic and its staff, the only reason she survives is due to a blessing from "the Gods."

The catastrophic IED blast sends Jacqueline home and her new outlook on life makes her reexamine her romantic history with the two men she's loved most — American soldier Elliott Wagner and French Defense Health Service psychiatrist Philomé Abdullahi — as she decides who she will be now that her high adrenaline lifestyle has concluded.

In this medical/military romance, Jacqueline Saint-Ebène builds the family she never knew she wanted.